The Magic of the Cenotaph . . .

Lan Martak closed his eyes and felt the rush of power surround him. Senses he didn't know he possessed rose inside, welling up, providing him with control. He sculpted the almost palpable waves around him. The warm, engulfing waves rose higher. A moment of panic. Control. Another flicker, followed by an intensely brilliant flash.

The Cenotaph Road opened.

The adventure began . . .

CENOTAPH ROAD #3
WORLD OF MAZES
ROBERT E. VARDEMAN

ACE SCIENCE FICTION BOOKS
NEW YORK

All characters in this book are fictitious.
Any resemblance to actual persons, living or dead,
is purely coincidental.

WORLD OF MAZES

An Ace Science Fiction Book/published by arrangement with
the author

PRINTING HISTORY
Ace Original/September 1983

ISBN: 0-441-91030-0

Ace Science Fiction Books are published by The Berkley Publishing Group,
200 Madison Avenue, New York, New York 10016.
PRINTED IN THE UNITED STATES OF AMERICA

CHAPTER ONE

"Die, fool, die!" screeched the sorcerer.

Lan Martak couldn't take his eyes off the ghastly sight hovering before him. Claybore had joined his severed, fleshless skull to the torso in the coffin. The combination gave the mage even more power. And shining brightly in the sorcerer's chest cavity was the Kinetic Sphere, that magical device allowing movement at will between different worlds. It pulsed pinkly, a heart for a being without mercy.

Lan felt the magics crackling and humming about him. Although Claybore lacked arms and hands to point a spell, his powers were awesome. The man felt as if a giant hand was crushing his chest, squeezing the breath from his lungs, ripping the life from his body. He had come to the top of majestic Mount Tartanius in hope of recovering the Kinetic Sphere; Claybore had gotten here first. Now Lan Martak's life was forfeit—and worse.

His giant spider companion, Krek, would also die with him. And Inyx, lovely Inyx, remained trapped between worlds. Without the Kinetic Sphere to free her, she would roam, more ghost than human, for all eternity, lost, alone, enduring pain beyond the realm of the physical.

He had failed, failed, failed.

The iron bands around Lan's chest tightened as Claybore augmented his spell. The immense altitude at the mountain-top did little in aiding Lan's gasping efforts to suck in more oxygen. Everything worked against him. Pinned like a bug in an entymologist's collection, he looked around the small stone shrine in panic. Krek, as tall and powerful as he was, couldn't help. Their other companions were likewise incapacitated. The ancient mage Abasi-Abi lay dying on the floor. His son Morto lacked any expertise in spell casting. And the fanatical pilgrim Ehznoll had been cast aside like a rag doll.

"Die, Lan Martak," crowed Claybore. The hollows where eyes had once resided in his skull glowed a dull red. At any moment twin beams of ruby death would surge forth and snuff out life.

Lan fought. In vain. The rejoining of skull with torso had given Claybore too much power.

The man felt life slipping from his body. The death beams wouldn't be needed.

A scream of rage and indignation from Ehznoll gave Lan a spurt of energy to resist. The pilgrim rose, obviously in extreme agony, and rushed toward the floating form of the sorcerer.

"Blasphemer!" cried Ehznoll. His mindless charge sent him smashing into the sorcerer. Claybore shrieked obscenities, then diabolical spells—but it was too late. The pilgrim's momentum carried human and human parody over the rim of the mountain. The instant Claybore vanished from sight, the spell lifted from Lan Martak.

He gasped, recovered, then dashed forward. Tumbling over and over, Ehznoll slowly vanished from sight. Alongside the pilgrim spun a pink pulsation. Lan tensed. A brilliant flare seared his eyes. He raised a hand to shield his vision from the light; Claybore had used the

Kinetic Sphere glowing in his cold chest cavity to switch worlds.

Lan Martak lived. But he had also failed. Now he had to face that soul-devouring fact every day of his life. Time passed, and Lan Martak didn't notice. Like a man drugged, he sat and stared over the rim of Mount Tartanius down into the mists below where so much of his life had just vanished. Inyx was similarly lost. Trapped between worlds, the woman was destined to roam, deserted and alone, forever. And, while this was a pleasant enough world, Lan had tasted the thrill of walking the Cenotaph Road, of finding and exploring new worlds. For most of his life he'd been trapped on a single world; following the advice of an ancient being, he'd taken a first hesitant step along the Road. He'd lost a love, killed an enemy, and found friends beyond compare in Krek and Inyx.

And they'd used the Kinetic Sphere to explore. Now that Claybore had regained his magical gateway, nothing prevented him from marching on defenseless, unsuspecting worlds and conquering them. His grey-clad soldiers would pour forth through the gate opened by the Kinetic Sphere and bring ruin and slavery to untold cultures.

Lan Martak stared down the side of Mount Tartanius, wondering if he should follow the valiant Ehznoll's path. One step, nothing, falling, death.

A light touch startled him.

"No, friend Lan Martak," came Krek's soft words. "That is Ehznoll's way, not yours. He died for his belief, for the betrayal of his faith. You must live for yours."

"Everything's gone. There's no way off this world. You said so yourself. Unless . . ." Hope leaped in his breast.

"No," said the coppery-furred arachnid, "I have discovered no other cenotaph off this world. With the Sphere gone, the 'vision' is clearer. There are no cenotaphs on this planet opening to other worlds, though I see countless ones opening onto it. These are one-way gates. Many have entered this world only to find no way off."

Lan slumped again. "Ehznoll's way may have been easier, but you're right. It's not my way." Looking up at the spider, he asked, "How's Abasi-Abi? The battle severely injured him."

"Worse. His son Morto tends him, as is proper."

"Maybe my healing spells can do something for him."

Inside the stone building, Morto knelt beside his father. The sorcerer had aged incredibly. Hair totally white, face lined as if some farmer had plowed it, transparent yellowed skin pulled across his hands as taut as a drumhead, he had come as close to death as possible without crossing the line.

"Here he is," said Morto quietly. To Lan, "He wishes to speak. But hurry. He is almost gone."

Lan cradled the old sorcerer's head.

"I didn't know," explained Lan. "I thought all Claybore wanted was the Sphere. I see it all now. He's rebuilding his body."

"You didn't know," absolved Abasi-Abi. "But for that ignorance you must now be punished." Lan tensed. "I am dying. You must carry on my fight against the evil Claybore promises. Morto will give you my grimoire. You have the native skill my son lacks in magic. You will learn all the spells you can to stop Claybore."

"He used the Kinetic Sphere to shift worlds," Lan said glumly. "I saw the flash as he opened the gateway. Do you think he'll be back to slay the rest of us?"

"No, because he thinks I am dead and you helpless. He thinks there is no way off this world."

"There's a way? Tell me!"

"First, I must tell you of Terrill." Abasi-Abi's voice barely reached Lan now. The man bent down so the dying whispers sounded directly in his ear. "He was a mighty sorcerer, the mightiest and now long dead. But he saw the evil Claybore brought. Only Terrill possessed the skill to stop Claybore—not kill him, no one can do that, but stop him."

"Is Terrill the one who dismembered Claybore and scattered the pieces along the Cenotaph Road?"

"Yes."

"Claybore cannot be killed, but he can be stopped? He needs his full body for full power?"

"Yes," whispered Abasi-Abi. "Only the skull is potent; with the body it is an even more potent pairing, but even this combination can be defeated. The danger lies in allowing Claybore to find the arms, legs, feet, hands. Once they are joined, no mage lives on any of the worlds able to withstand Claybore's might."

"You'll live, Abasi-Abi. I'll start my healing spells. They aren't much, but . . ."

"No!" Bony fingers clawed at Lan's arm.

"I'll have you back on your feet again. Soon. I promise."

"Lan," said Morto in a peculiarly flat voice. "He's dead. He fought death, tried to deny it. No one can do that, not even one as powerful as my father."

Lan Martak placed the lifeless body gently on the soft floor.

"He didn't tell me how to get off this world. He wanted to tell me about Terrill and Claybore, but he never said anything about leaving here."

"Here is his grimoire. He wanted you to have it." Morto passed over a small volume bound in brown leather and brass. Lan took it gingerly, as if it would bite.

"It's yours. You're his son."

"I cannot use it. I have no talent at all for magic, much to his disgust." Emotion returned to Morto's voice and color rose in his blanched cheeks. "He was a harsh master and an unloving father." Tears choked him now. He made no attempt to hide his sorrow. "But still I loved him and believed in what he had to do."

Together the three of them, two human and one arachnid, buried the sorcerer. The glassy plain of Mount Tartanius' mesa proved hard to dig in, but the combined assault of

Lan's sword and Krek's talons, with Morto's blind determination, finally cut the grave.

Lan Martak spent the next four days studying Abasi-Abi's notebook. One spell in the grimoire sent Lan's heart racing. He composed himself, allowed the immense tides of magic flowing between worlds to suffuse his body, then cast himself outward. Like the *therra* on his home world, his spirit left his body and he roamed. Hours passed as he searched, disembodied, for Inyx. The world around his roving spirit, changed to a featureless plain, finally became the impenetrable white fog he'd experienced before.

"Inyx!" he called. No answer. "Inyx, I need to reach you. I need you."

"Lan?" A voice, hesitant, distant.

"Inyx! Are you all right?"

"I . . . feel . . . so . . . light. No . . . body. I . . . remain in . . . this place . . . too long."

The voice faded. Lan never caught sight of the woman but heard the fear in her words. Once he imagined the brush of fingers across his, but he shook that off as wishful thinking. He'd been told that to remain too long in the white fogginess robbed a mortal of body and left behind only tortured spirit. It was true, and Inyx knew it.

He had to rescue her and didn't know how.

His spirit returned to his body. The weakness hitting him made Lan gasp and collapse. For two days Morto and Krek tended him. The excursion had been costly for him, both in energy and morale.

"I don't see how we can do it. Not on the top of this thrice-damned mountain."

"Friend Lan Martak, there must be a way. Abasi-Abi hinted as much."

"Hints, Krek, don't mean a thing. The man was dying."

"Inyx remains in limbo."

"Dammit, I know." Spots of red flushed Lan's cheeks.

He paced constantly, Abasi-Abi's spell book open in one hand. "I've gone over the contact spells again and again. They don't work for me. I don't have the experience, the control, the *knowledge*."

"While I am no mage, reading through this one indicates a path to follow." Krek's front right claw tapped the book, opened on the stone altar in the hut.

"That's a spell for creating a cenotaph. Yes, maybe the creation would bring Inyx out of the fog, but I can't do it."

"Why not?"

Lan snorted in disgust.

"I lack the most essential ingredient for a cenotaph: a dead hero."

"There is one."

"Abasi-Abi won't work. We've buried him already. The grave must be freshly consecrated with those spells— and the hero's body must be irretrievably lost."

"Such as lost, meaning not recoverable?"

Sometimes the spider could be so dense Lan wanted to scream.

"Yes, lost. Like . . . oh, no. Of course."

"Like Ehznoll," they chorused.

"How could I have overlooked it, Krek? He died saving us—the world—from Claybore. When he hit the ground below, nothing but pink splotches would have been left, and those would be smeared halfway down the mountain. We can consecrate a cenotaph to Ehznoll!"

"Obvious."

Lan spent a half-hour chiding himself for not seeing the obvious, then took another hour worrying about the qualities of Ehznoll's heroism. He finally decided heroism, no matter how motivated, provided the intense psychic energy required for establishing the Cenotaph Road. The gateway between worlds could be opened, no matter what he'd thought of Ehznoll while he lived.

Lan Martak pored over the spells while Krek and

Morto hollowed out the altar inside the hut. A special crypt had to be formed, one large enough to hold a human—or spider. But for all his bulk and eight long, furry legs, Krek managed easily to compact himself down into large human size.

As the spider and human finished their chore, Lan said, "The preliminary spells are ready. I . . . I've improvised." He looked from Krek to Morto, to see if they approved.

"Improvised in what way?" asked Morto.

"I've sent a seeking spell into the whiteness and tried to couple it with the opening of the cenotaph. In this way, as the Cenotaph Road opens, Inyx will be pulled along and deposited on the proper world—the world onto which the cenotaph joins this one. We follow and join her."

He sighed, thinking of being with Inyx once again. They had been apart for too long.

"Which world?" the man asked.

"Which? Well, I can't say for sure. Is there any way of telling beforehand?"

"There is. My father often cast scrying spells for days hunting for the exact world he desired most."

"I can't do that. It . . . it wasn't in his book." Lan again felt his inadequacy as a mage. All through his preparations he'd sensed his control teetering, almost being lost. The energies he moulded were immense and immensely beyond his comprehension. Still, necessity forced him into the role of sorcerer.

"Are we going to the world Claybore shifted to?" asked Krek.

"I don't know. There's so much about this I just don't know."

"Fear naught, friend Lan Martak. You have done well, I am sure. Though I do remember the time when you . . ." The spider's voice trailed off in memory of some gaffe on Lan's part.

"The spells. Now." Lan Martak closed his eyes and felt the rush of power surround him. As if he stood on a beach and the ocean waves lapped around his ankles, the power mounted. Up to his knees. Control. He fought to prevent a runaway of the energies he commanded. To his waist. A *flicker*. The gateway almost opened. Senses he didn't know he possessed rose inside, welling up and providing him with control. He sculpted the almost palpable waves around him. The Cenotaph Road beckoned. The warm, engulfing waves rose higher, ever higher. To his neck. Over his head. A moment of panic. Control. He regained control. Another *flicker*, followed by an intensely brilliant *flash*.

The Cenotaph Road opened.

The waves receded from around him. Lan didn't simply let loose. He maintained control as long as possible, nurturing the energy, stroking it as if it were a thing alive, coaxing the most possible from it. The cenotaph had been opened to another world, but an important element still remained unfulfilled.

Inyx.

"Come closer. Come to me. Follow the light from the Road," he called into the whiteness.

"Lan, so near. I'm coming. Wait for me. Wait!"

"Inyx!"

He blinked and stared into the yawning crypt carved into the stone altar. A misty form appeared, shimmered, started to vanish. He *reached* out and manipulated the energies and prevented Inyx's departure. The form coalesced into a woman. She lay in the crypt, confusion on her face. She turned, tried to sit up. The narrow confines prevented her from doing more than straightening her long legs.

"Inyx, you're back. Thank all . . . Inyx!"

"Lan!"

She reached out, touched his hand, then disappeared with a loud snapping noise.

"What happened? Krek, she was here and I lost her. She's back in the mist."

"No, friend Lan Martak. She didn't go back. I watched carefully. She retained her material body, and, by human standards, a nice one it is, too. I prefer more fur on the legs, naturally. All arachnids enjoy the sight of several well-turned legs, those being our most prominent feature.''

"Krek!"

"Oh, yes. As I was saying, she formed most nicely, then winked out of sight. I do believe the cenotaph opened and took her. She walked the Road.''

"It opened already? Of course it did. I opened it!''

"And it has already closed. Remember, the cenotaphs do not remain open constantly. Only once daily do they open, then for an appallingly short period. You should look into changing that, the next cenotaph you make.''

"It's closed?'' Lan hardly believed his ears. The first crypt he'd entered had been open to another world for only seconds. This one consecrated to Ehznoll had been open for long minutes—but he'd taken those minutes to summon Inyx, to coax her from the whiteness. By the time she'd reposed in the crypt, the time had expired.

Inyx travelled ahead of them to a new world. They had to wait for another day to follow.

"We're still not together!'' he complained.

"There is only time between the two of you now,'' said Morto. "Wait a day, then follow. She saw you and must know that you follow. She will wait at the other side.''

"Wait,'' said Lan glumly. "So we wait.''

Inyx drifted, any real substance just beyond her fingertips. Every time she gripped down, she felt only . . . mist. The all-pervasive whiteness wrapped her like damp, fleecy cotton wool. She fought against it, thrashing, cursing, struggling. Only the slight wetness of fog greeted her.

"Inyx!'' came the distant cry. She turned, trying to recognize the voice, trying to decide from what direction it came.

"Lan!'' she screamed. "I'm over here! Help me! I don't know where I am!''

The voice calling her name grew fainter. She panicked.

Ever since Claybore had trapped them between worlds, she had been wandering alone. Other wraiths in the white mistiness passed close by, but she had avoided them. They weren't—quite—human. This limbo had been reserved for the damned souls unable to find rest. Lan's voice gave her the first hope she'd had since entering this nothingness.

"Inyx . . . stay where . . . you are. I . . . come."

She saw a brief flash of brown hair, the color a riot of sensation after the continual diet of white. Lan Martak turned and faced her. Her hands reached out, brushed over—*through*—his. Inyx cried in frustration when the man faded away.

But hope had been reborn in her breast. Lan still sought her. He hadn't abandoned her. That thought made the waiting easier. A little bit, at least.

She might have stood for an instant or centuries. Inyx had no way of deciding how long it had been between sighting Lan and the feeling of being sucked into a vortex. Slight tuggings pulled at her ankles, her legs, her body. She turned and cried out as her misty body began spinning in a miniature tornado.

Hardness rubbed her arms and back. Suffused light shone in her eyes. Detail came into the world. She rested in a stone crypt, the top pulled away to reveal an eight-foot-tall spider and a haggard man, his eyes shining with feral brilliance and a shock of sweat-soaked brown hair swaying across his forehead.

"Lan!" Inyx sat up in the crypt, reaching out to him. "You . . ." Her words trailed off as the vertigo she associated with walking the Cenotaph Road took possession of her senses, spinning her around and making her feel as if she'd been turned inside out. "No!" she cried piteously, but the protest echoed hollowly inside the rugged stone crypt, now turned dark and dank.

She sniffed the air, then coughed. Mildew had attacked the stone, giving a musty odor. Inyx shoved upward against rough stone and felt the lid to the crypt begin to slowly

grate away. Using muscles that had been inactive for—
how long?—caused aches to assert themselves. The dark-
haired woman loved the feel.

A body! She was out of the white limbo and back in the
real world. But which world? Somehow, Lan had created a
cenotaph to get her out of the nothingness between worlds.
He had also miscalculated the opening time. She had
escaped her private, dimensionless hell but had been tossed
at random along the Cenotaph Road.

Muscles tensed as she sat half-upright and pushed harder
against the stone. It didn't matter which world this cenotaph opened onto. Lan and Krek would follow as soon as
theirs opened once again. They would be with her. The
three of them together!

Inyx rejoiced.

The starry heavens above displayed constellations unfa-
miliar to her. Cool dew moistened her forehead, and the
heady scent of pine forest came from close by. Soft winds
whispered through the treetops and came to caress her
face, sensuously touching her face, throat, breasts. She
lived and rejoiced in every sensation. For too long, she
had been deprived of all of them. Sitting up, she saw dark
forms moving nearby. Humans, from the sound of their
motion and the words they uttered.

"Greetings," she called out, anxious once again to be
with anyone not a ghost. Inyx pulled herself to her feet,
still in the crypt. As her eyes adjusted to the night's
darkness, she felt a cold lump forming in the pit of her
stomach.

The men she faced were all grey-clad soldiers. They
ringed her in. She had escaped Claybore's curse in the
whiteness to find his army's might in another world. Inyx
was trapped.

CHAPTER TWO

"The time is almost upon us," said Krek. "Prepare to follow through the cenotaph."

"I'm ready," said Lan. "Are you, Morto?"

"No."

"What?"

"I'm not going." The dead mage's son stood to one side of the hut, his chin held high and a glow about him that Lan had never seen before. He appeared more confident now, his shoulders straighter and his face composed. For too long he had lived in his father's long shadow. Morto obviously had come to a decision on his own now, possibly for the first time. Free of familial obligation, he grew as a man.

"Why not?"

"I will stay on this world. Others offer me nothing I can't find here."

"And?"

"I would carry on Ehznoll's religion. The strength of this cenotaph is a tribute to his courage. There must have been parts of his belief more potent than any magic. Perhaps faith is always stronger. It is something I must explore for my own peace of mind. Also, my father lies on this mountain; I think my destiny does, also.''

"Come with us, Morto. Don't spend your life in this way. Help us continue your father's fight against Claybore.''

"My fight lies elsewhere. I haven't the talent or will to do battle with Claybore. Let me stay and tend to this holy shrine. It is something I can do, something I want to do. Go, go find your friend.''

"The cenotaph opens, friend Lan Martak.'' The giant spider jumped nervously from one side to the other, his long, furry legs knotting with eagerness to go through the world-shifting cenotaph.

"Morto?''

"Go.''

Lan's blossoming magical sense "saw" the cenotaph begin to open. It glowed like a brightly lit doorway leading into a far better place. Krek momentarily blocked off the light, then vanished. Through the illuminated rectangle Lan saw a new world, a world completely different from the barren, glassy plain atop Mount Tartanius. He glanced back at Morto to see another kind of light, a religious fervor such as had sent Ehznoll plunging to his death.

Lan never hesitated. With the litheness of youth, he vaulted into the crypt and immediately lay down. Less than a second elapsed before the magics he had released began taking hold of his mind and body. He started to call out in joy that his spells actually worked. He experienced a vertigo of the world-shifting, but it was a familiar sensation now. Lan calmed and blinked, opening his eyes to see Krek looming high above the new crypt. Luckily the spider had removed the lid and gotten free; otherwise, the fit trying to get both of them into the same coffin-sized space would have been too tight for comfort.

"It is night,'' said Krek. "Almost dawn.''

"Inyx, where's Inyx?'' Lan demanded. He forced his

way past the crouching spider, worming his way through
the legs imprisoning him in the cenotaph.

No Inyx.

"She's not here," he said, crestfallen.

"There is no way to know how long it has been since
she arrived," said the spider.

"But it's only a day."

"It was only a day for us. Time moves strangely on
different worlds. She might have been here a week already.
She might have decided we were not coming and gone
exploring on her own."

"She wouldn't do that," protested Lan. But in his heart
he knew Krek was probably right. Inyx lacked patience.
She might have decided that they could follow her when
they arrived.

Krek jumped out and lightly dropped into soft earth
beside the gravesite. He bobbed up and down, canting his
head to one side while thinking his spiderish thoughts. Lan
didn't bother asking what those thoughts were. He began
circling the cenotaph, studying the ground, looking for a
sign indicating where Inyx might be. He had fought too
long and hard and had gone through too many tribulations
to give up easily on her.

So close. Back on Mount Tartanius she had been just
inches away before the magic of the cenotaph transported
her here.

His magics, his cenotaphs. Lan Martak cursed himself
for not understanding better the magics contained in Abasi-
Abi's brown leather-bound grimoire. His hand touched the
book carefully tucked away inside his tunic. The lore of
the ages rested in that small book. Learning it wouldn't be
an overnight task. Abasi-Abi had spent his life growing in
power; when he faced Claybore, that knowledge had only
delayed his final fate.

Lan dropped to hands and knees and examined a scuffed
area in the dirt.

"Krek, look at this. A group of men were here, perhaps

three or four days ago. The weathering of their footprints shows as much.''

"There has not been any rain," said the spider. "For which I am thankful. How ugly having water fall from the sky and mat the fur on your legs."

"The prints, Krek," said Lan, bringing his friend's attention back to the ground.

"Ah, yes, the prints. A dozen soldiers."

"All the imprints are the same," said Lan, feeling a coldness creeping up inside. If the men waiting around had been the usual ragtag band of itinerants, their boots would have different markings. All these heelprints were identical, with the only difference being the size of the sole. Soldiers.

"There is some small sign of Inyx. There." The spider pointed using one of his long legs.

"Yes, that might be Inyx's," said Lan, "but we can't tell. It's different, but it's been stepped on too many times."

"She might be in the hands of the grey-clad soldiers."

"Or maybe these are local militia." Lan said it and didn't believe it. Claybore's skills were vast. He might have felt the creation of a new cenotaph leading off Mount Tartanius. If so, it was a small matter to send a company of soldiers to watch this site. When Inyx emerged, the soldiers captured her.

And he had been the one sending her directly into their arms.

"Nothing I do is right," Lan lamented.

"The creation of this cenotaph was well done. You still learn, and we do battle with a powerful mage. All in all, you have not done badly. With a few exceptions."

"I don't want to hear about it," said Lan, cutting off the itemized list of his failures. He knew them only too well. Each and every one burned like a fresh wound in his mind.

"The soldiers," said Krek, moving about in a rocking motion, his tiny head bobbing and mandibles clacking ferociously, "went this way. Shall we, also?"

Lan checked to be sure his sword slipped easily in its sheath, then began his long, ground-eating stride in the direction Krek had indicated. It might have been a day or a week before that the woman had come through the cenotaph, but now only distance separated Inyx from them.

"The world is full of game, good forests teeming with edible plants, everything we could want." Lan lounged back and stared up into the cloudless blue sky. For two days they'd tramped along, following the trail left by the small patrol of grey-clads. The lack of any indication that Inyx was with them made Lan a little uneasy, but this seemed their only choice. He carefully examined the tracks at every point along the way, hoping for some sign showing the woman's presence, and finding none. He went forward on hope alone.

"What a singularly annoying sound," said Krek. The spider hunkered down into a lumpy brown mass next to a tree. "The shrieking sounds pierce my ears."

At first Lan didn't hear anything. It finally came to him, distant, high-pitched. He scanned the clear sky and found two dots weaving and darting about. Squinting, he saw tiny jets of flame lancing from the rear of each spot.

"Whatever can that be?" Lan felt an uneasiness as the dots grew in size, coming closer. His burgeoning sense of magic twinged like an arthritic knee before a rainstorm.

"They move too quickly to be gliders."

"But they are under human control."

"They certainly would not be under arachnid control," sniffed Krek. "No self-respecting spider would ever enter such a dangerous flying contraption."

The dots grew in size until Lan made out details. Metallic, the craft sported short wings on either side and had mark-

ings indicating opposing sides in some unknown war. The
craft engaged in swiftly paced aerial combat. Long lances
of eye-searing violet flame lashed from the back, somehow
propelling the craft and keeping it airborne. As the craft
maneuvered for position, huge gouts of fire lashed forward
in attempts to engulf the other craft. Lan noticed that, as
the front of the craft spewed forth flame, it shuddered and
slowed. Only when the forward fires died did the speed
pick up again.

"An odd form of combat. One totally not to my liking,"
said Krek. "You humans manage to find the most diabolical ways of killing yourselves of any species I have encountered along the Cenotaph Road. It is a wonder you are
proliferating so while displaying such vicious, self-destructive
tendencies."

"The one has a skull emblem on the side. Do you
think . . . ?" Even before Lan got the words from his mouth,
that craft swerved, seemed to slide sideways in the air, and
got behind the other craft. Flames danced forward, searing
the enemy's tail section. Lan winced when he saw the
result. The craft in front blasted apart in midair.

"A fire elemental," he said in awe. "I read about them
in Abasi-Abi's grimoire, but even he lacked the spells to
properly contain them." In midair danced the now-released
propulsive system of the doomed craft. The elemental
shrieked in glee at being freed and arrowed straight up and
out of sight. Its shrill cries of freedom rang in Lan's ears
long after it had gone.

"The craft comes down nearby."

"The man inside," said Lan. "He'll be killed if he
stays with it."

The metallic bird tumbled and pitched, pieces cartwheel-
ing away as it descended. Lan saw the pilot push back a
transparent hatch, then vault into air, seemingly to his
death. Lan's heart almost stopped—then he felt intense
magics forming again.

Air sucked away from where he stood, rushed together, and formed a vortex surging upward into the sky. The cyclone caught up the man flailing about in midair and tossed him back into the sky. Battered by the high winds generated by the air elemental but pulled inexorably by gravity, the man slowly came to earth.

Long before his feet touched the ground, the remnants of his craft smashed into the forest not a hundred yards from Lan and Krek. Lan glanced up at the pilot, still whirling around in his personal storm, then ran for the downed and smouldering craft. His curiosity overpowered his desire to help the man.

Krek followed until they came within a few feet of the craft. Hot metallic smells filled the air. The craft's tail section had vanished and one wing had been ripped off in the descent. The cramped quarters where the pilot had crouched rested above a thick tube running the length of the craft.

"That's how they did it," marvelled Lan. "They trapped the fire elemental. The rushing heat expelled from the rear shoved the craft forward, but when the pilot wanted to attack, he opened up the front end of the chamber holding the elemental. Flame rushed forward, along the tube the pilot straddled. The elemental's heat gushed out to spray the enemy craft."

"How interesting," Krek said testily. "The air is not fit for breathing. The metallic tang is much too unpleasant." The spider bounced away a few paces.

"But how did he generate the air elemental to get him safely to the ground?" Lan wondered out loud. "What sorcerers this world must have! Maybe we can find some to oppose Claybore and stop him before he grows too powerful."

"You dream, friend Lan Martak."

"What?"

"This incident indicates a war. The skull emblem on the

side of the victor might hint that Claybore already rules this world."

The man looked at the blistered insignia on the side of the downed craft: a fist holding a dagger. What Krek said might be true.

"The only way of finding out is to ask."

They ran for the middle of the field where the air elemental still kicked up a choking column of dust. The pilot of the craft had collapsed in a pile in the center of the rotating windstorm. Lan ignored Krek's pleas to give up this mad quest and find a nice, peaceful spot where the wind didn't rip at furry legs, and pushed inward.

The pilot, more dead than alive, struggled for a moment.

"It's all right," soothed Lan. "I'm not going to hurt you. Tell me what happened."

"The grey army. Th-their air arm is too strong. Too good."

"You fight the grey-clad soldiers?"

A single nod.

"How much of this world have they taken over?"

"Almost all," came the disheartening answer. "Only small bands of resistance remain. The howler, the one I flew, it was our last. We are grounded now."

"Howler? You mean the craft holding the fire elemental?"

Again a single nod. The man weakened visibly.

"Is Claybore here?"

Incomprehension.

"The leader of the grey-clad soldiers. Is he personally on this world? My friends and I fight him. We would join with your group. Tell me how we can do that." The man tensed, then sagged. "Tell me!" raged Lan. He realized the man had died. Ugly burns on the man's left side had been the cause of death. The pain must have been excruciating. Claybore's aerial craft had done too good a job at killing.

Lan allowed the man's head to sink into the soft earth. He had made his last landing.

"We'll stop Claybore," he promised the dead pilot. "We will." He rose and turned to Krek. The winds from the air elemental had died to a soft breeze, but that breeze had masked the sounds of approaching men. High overhead Claybore's howler rocked back and forth in salute, then shrieked off, the captive elemental protesting mightily at the exertion.

Circling Lan were twenty grey-clad soldiers. Krek had already been captured.

CHAPTER THREE

For a moment, Inyx and the soldiers stood staring at one another in disbelief. They hadn't drawn their weapons, and she was too surprised to move. She recovered her wits first.

Diving, twisting, she succeeded in getting past the one closest to her. His powerful hands grabbed and caught the fabric of her tunic, but his grip and her determination to leave were stronger than the cloth. It ripped, leaving him holding only a swath of useless cloth. Boots scuffled in the dust and she heard the soldiers' growing confusion. She had a chance. As she ran for the shelter of the pine trees nearby, she pulled her sword.

"Who is she?" demanded one of the soldiers behind her.

"What difference does it make? We were ordered to stop anyone coming out of this cenotaph. So what if she doesn't fit the description Silvain gave us? Get her!" The words convinced her that Claybore's soldiers waited for Lan and Krek, not her. Claybore didn't know she had been freed from the white limbo between worlds. As Inyx ran for cover, she debated the wisdom of trying to eliminate all the men around the grave. Something gnawed at the fringes of her mind and kept her from turning and challenging them.

She finally found a small hummock behind which to hide. Panting, she slowly controlled her racing heart and got herself under better control. Sword in hand, she waited. The soldiers blundered about in the dark until their leader finally called them back. For a few minutes, nothing happened, then light blazed forth.

One of the soldiers held aloft an iron cage. Trapped inside was a small demon, valiantly blazing and casting light in all directions. Whenever the light began to fade, the soldier holding the cage rapped the bars sharply with a stick.

"Don't you dare turn off," warned the soldier. "You know what I'll do to you."

"Not the buckets of water," moaned the tiny demon. "Please, not that. They put me out for days!"

"Then give us more light!"

The demon obliged. Inyx got her first good look at the men in the band. There remained no doubt that these were more of Claybore's troops. They wore the same cut of uniform, had the same arcane red sleeve markings indicating rank. Most of all their arrogance marked them. But what struck the woman as odd was the lack of weapons at their belts. None carried a sword, and only one or two had daggers. In place of the more familiar weapon rested small tubes. Inyx knew little about magic but guessed that those cylinders must be formidable, indeed, to replace a razor-sharp longsword.

Glancing around, she studied the lay of the land to get some idea of an escape route. The soldiers still milled about uncertainly. Their leader seemed tossed on the horns of a dilemma. A solitary woman had come through instead of a brown-haired man and a giant spider. Did this make her important to Claybore, or should the troops wait for their designated victims?

She didn't give their captain time to decide. Moving as quietly as shadow across shadow, Inyx slipped deeper into the forest. The woman relished the feel of earth beneath her feet again, the invigorating scent of pine needles, the feel of sap sticking to her fingers as she lightly touched a rough tree trunk. She almost lost herself to sensation when she detected a small, plaintive cry for help.

Not believing her ears, Inyx moved even more cautiously. Behind, in the depths of the forest, she heard the grey-clad soldiers blundering about. They had little training for this type of tracking. She wondered at that, just as she wondered at their odd weapons.

"Help me, oh, please, some kind, generous Samaritan, help me!"

She edged around a large-boled tree and stared in disbelief into a small clearing. A metallic vessel of a type she'd never before seen rested in the center. The voice came not from the compartment in front but from the rear portion. In spite of her need for caution, Inyx found herself more curious than careful. She advanced.

"Who's there?" came the immediate response, suspicious, terse. "Who is it?"

"My name is Inyx. Does that mean anything to you?" The woman figured that Claybore already knew her; giving her name now meant nothing. She had never believed in magics requiring a name to act.

"No, can't say that it does. Will you release me? Those fiends! They've kept me in here for years. I mean, positively, for *years*."

"Where are you?" She looked around the oddity and finally scratched her head in bemusement. She had no idea at all what she'd found. Inyx poked the side of the hull with her sword. Definitely metal. A small door swung away to allow someone to enter the compartment, but why anyone desired that course was beyond her. Only a simple, uncomfortable wooden seat and a single stick protruding from the floor were visible in the tiny iron cell.

"In the back, of course."

She looked. To the rear of the craft was a door with an elaborate lock on it. Inyx had seen similar devices before. This not only mechanically barred entry, it magically barred exit. Whatever was trapped in the metal hull needed more than simple physical bonds.

"You're a demon," she accused. "They've trapped you inside for a reason."

"A reason, yes," came the baleful reply. "They misuse me so! I simply cannot stand another instant of this durance vile. I'll go insane, quite insane, I tell you."

Inyx peered into a small port drilled through the door. Less than an inch away, peering back at her, was a large bloodshot eye with catlike slitted pupils. She straightened, then peeked back inside. The demon had moved away, allowing a clearer view. The magically trapped creature hunkered down on scaly haunches. She estimated its total size to be less than six inches from the spiked tip of its pointy head to the taloned claws on its lizard feet. A forked tongue slithered out, only to sneak back between black lips. Tiny hands gestured frantically.

"Help me escape. They are so cruel to me."

Inyx had some experience with such creatures in her wanderings along the Cenotaph Road and knew better than to believe anything the demon said. Once released, this tiny, insignificant demon might sprout to a hundred times its current size. Without knowing the nature of the spell binding it inside, she dared not meddle.

"Why do they imprison you?"

"To do their bidding."

"Which is?"

"Operate this craft, of course. Isn't that simply dreadful? They abuse and overwork me. I mean, it's worse than shovelling shit in the fiery pit, don't you agree?"

"What do you do?"

"They make me spin this." One of the ineffectual hands reached out and touched a vertical shaft fitted with ribbed vanes. "It's hard work for one my size."

"You must be very powerful," she said, still not understanding what the demon actually did.

"Very. I've been trapped here, against my will, mind you, for almost forty years. And all so they can have their fun. It's enough to drive me over the edge, it really is."

"Show me what you do. Maybe I can think of something to aid you."

"You will? You'll help me get away from them? They are *ever* so mean, you know."

Inyx watched through the tiny port as the demon began spinning the shaft. Slowly at first, it turned the shaft. Huffing and puffing noxious fumes, it worked the shaft faster and faster. A whining sound filled the air. Startled, Inyx looked up. Four metal blades had unfurled from the rotor protruding from the top of the hull. They snapped out longer than two of her strides and began spinning. The tiny wind whipping at her dark hair grew into a tornado.

"Get in. I'll take you away from here. Then you can release me," said the demon. "I hear them returning. I just know I'm not making a mistake trusting you. You look like such a dear, sweet person. You won't fail me, will you?"

"Get in?" asked Inyx. "But . . ." the sound of the soldiers tromping through the dry underbrush finally reached her less sensitive ears. The demon had given her ample warning to run. With the forest-lore shown already by the soldiers, she'd have no trouble eluding them, perhaps succeeding in reducing their rank in the process.

But the lure of curiosity egged her on to do something foolish. She jumped into the cramped front compartment and slammed shut the transparent door.

"The stick. Take the stick and put it between your legs, dear lady." The demon tittered as it spoke.

Glaring, Inyx did as she was told. Immediately, the craft lifted. She screamed at the sensation of rising so precipitously. Clutching frantically at the stick with both hands, she pulled it toward her in a naive attempt to correct what she saw as a problem. The craft lurched and the nose turned up to face the grey light of dawn.

"Down!" screamed the demon from behind her. "Keep the damned nose level!"

Inyx controlled her fear to obey. The demon's advice proved just the thing to quiet her fear. As long as she maintained a relative equilibrium, the craft didn't flutter up and down like a butterfly or swing from side to side.

"They don't have many like this one left," the demon said proudly. "All the sorcerers have left Dicca. Can't stand that scum, our dear, elected Lord of the Twistings."

"Lord of the Twistings?"

"You aren't from around here, are you, sweetie?" asked the demon. Its tone changed slightly. Inyx tensed.

"What difference does that make? I'm still your best bet for freedom."

"True. But where are you from? Not that dreary island of Sala Tria. I had to fly out there once. Some bigshot convention of leaders. The Lord of the Twistings was positively rude to so many of them. Why they took it from that wimp, I'll never know. Just because he can . . ."

"Can what?"

"Never mind that."

"Take me to Dicca," Inyx commanded. "Then I'll see about getting you out of that compartment."

"Dicca? You *really* want to go to Dicca?"

"Why not? Anything wrong with going there?"

"No, no," the demon said hastily. "It's one of my all-time forever favorite spots." Inyx wondered what was wrong with the city, if Dicca actually was a city.

"Because that's where the sorcerers imprisoned you?"

"That was a long time ago. This isn't my first fluttercraft assignment. I've worn out a couple." Inyx peered into a small hole directly above her right shoulder. She got another view of the demon dutifully twisting the rotor that kept the blades spinning outside at a speed fast enough to force air down and keep the craft aloft. Tiny bands of steel muscle stood out on the demon's forearms and shoulders. The immense strength shown convinced her against ever letting it free. Such power turned easily.

"Tell me about Dicca. Why have all the sorcerers left it?"

"Those smelly grey-clad soldiers, why else do you think? They barge in and take over. Some sorcerer with more balls than any of those around Dicca is backing them, you can count on it. He's got all the local talent scared so much they pee pink."

"Claybore?"

"Might be. Haven't heard that name. I know that it was Nnamdi-lo who locked me up for the first time. When I get out of this chamberpot, I'm going to—"

"Keep up speed," ordered Inyx. The demon's momentary lapse into describing what it would do to its jailer had permitted a slackening in airspeed. She felt the fluttercraft hesitate slightly and begin to lose altitude. They were only a few feet over the tallest of the trees. Any lower spelled a nasty collision with the upper branches.

Experimenting, Inyx pulled back on the stick. The craft nosed up. She levelled out at a safer altitude.

"You handle this like you were born to it," said the demon. "You're not lying to me, are you, sweetie? You *will* let me go when we reach Dicca?"

"Why shouldn't I?"

"You might be one of them. All they do is lie. Promises mean nothing, I can tell you."

"Dicca and freedom," Inyx said firmly.

"Freedom!" screamed the demon. The fluttercraft's speed picked up even more. Inyx watched the creature bend its diminutive back to the task of spinning the shaft. The whomp-whomp-whomp of the blades above gave her a headache, but she had to admit this mode of travel was far superior to walking.

Even better, she left Claybore's soldiers far behind.

"What a majestic city!" she exclaimed. The demon gave her an aerial tour of Dicca. They circumnavigated the boundaries, then worked inward in an ever-decreasing spiral. They passed over all but the palace in the center of the city.

"Nice, if you like . . ." The demon stopped in mid-sentence.

"Like what?"

"Like all those people," it finished lamely. Inyx wasn't fooled for a moment. The demon had started to say something else and had held back. They were sneaky beasts, but no more so than many humans she'd found in her walkings along the Road.

"Land me in a good place," she said, wondering where that might be. The city streets were often narrow and twisting. Maybe that lack of forethought on the city designer's part gave the title to the king or mayor or whatever function the Lord of the Twistings fulfilled.

"Dear lady, the park is where you want to go. Plenty of open spaces, green grass, the sky above, none of those piles of donkey dump to get in your way—"

"No travelogue, just a landing," she said. Inyx was more used to outdoors. Travelling in the cramped forward compartment of the fluttercraft made her feel a bit claustrophobic. Nothing she couldn't handle, but she wished for nothing more than open spaces again—and an end to the demon's incessant chattering.

"You're beginning to sound more and more like *them*," the demon said acerbically.

"Land."

The landing proved more of a crash. The demon simply stopped turning the rotor and allowed the fluttercraft to fall from an altitude of twenty feet. Inyx found herself bouncing around in the compartment like a peä in the hold of a storm-wracked ocean freighter. Hanging on to the control stick, she managed to keep from pitching forward through the front window. When the craft came to a final, slumping halt, she popped out, glad to be alive.

"Release me," came the plaintive cry from the rear. "I've done what you wanted, sweetie. Now keep your promise."

"I never promised," she said. Brushing a strand of jet-black hair back from her forehead, she considered her options. Simply leaving the demon imprisoned seemed the safest course. It might turn on her out of spite. They weren't noted for loyalty, at the least the ones she'd come across weren't. Still, she had led the creature to believe she would release it.

Her thoughts were interrupted by a gruff voice demanding, "Where's your spittin' landin' permit?"

Inyx turned to face a big-boned woman with stringy, bleached-blonde hair. The tattered dress only partially hid liver-spotted skin along the shoulders and upper arms and a few festering sores on bulging breasts. The woman wiped her nose along a flabby left forearm, then repeated her question.

"High and mighty, where's the landin' permit? You got one, ain'tcha?"

"Permit?"

"Dammit, another'un who thinks she's better'n the common folk." The burly woman spat a green gob that landed a few inches in front of Inyx's boots. She seemed to take no notice when Inyx half drew her sword. "I gotta keep the order 'round here, ain't I?"

"Let me out!" cried the demon.

"You promisin' something you can't deliver, big'uns?" the woman demanded of Inyx, eyeing her as if she were a slab of meat hanging on a butcher's hook. "Those real or did you get some love-besotted mage to grow 'em for ya?"

"Where do I get the landing permit?"

The woman hunched forward slightly and squinted at Inyx before answering.

"Take care of it for a fiver," she said.

"She's a thief!" called out the demon. "Landing fees are never more than a halver."

"I've got to get the money. From a friend. In the city."

"Humph," growled the woman, spitting again, "I just bet you gotta lot of friends. One every spittin' five minutes, I betcha. Don't care where you get the money—or how. Just get it and the permit. Till then, I watch over the fluttercraft."

"No!" protested the demon.

"All right," agreed Inyx.

"Let me out!"

"I'll be back within a half-hour," she told the burly woman.

"Don't go bruisin' that fine backside of yours hurryin' your friends along." The woman laughed at her crude comment. She again ignored Inyx's motion to draw her sword. Inyx relaxed and turned for the small footpath leading toward the nearest portion of tall buildings marking the perimeter of Dicca.

"No, I won't do it!" Inyx heard the demon exclaim. "She promised me!"

Inyx hadn't gone fifty feet when she heard the blades of the fluttercraft begin to whine and bite the air. The craft rose quickly and headed in the opposite direction. It was about what she'd expected. The obese woman may have been ignorant of soap, but she knew a great deal about thievery. She'd stolen the fluttercraft.

Inyx had to laugh. She'd taken care of two problems. The soldiers, if they pursued, might be led away by the other woman's theft. And it no longer was within her power to release the demon. She hadn't actually lied to it, after all.

She started down the path into Dicca. She had gone less than ten yards when she heard a low, deep-throated snarl. Spinning, Inyx faced one of the largest, hungriest-looking tigers she'd ever seen.

It advanced on her, fangs dripping in anticipation of a fine meal.

CHAPTER FOUR

Inyx froze. The slightest motion on her part meant instant death. The tiger's powerful shoulder muscles rippled with ill-suppressed eagerness. She didn't want to give the large cat any more reason to attack than she had to. Holding down her fear, she slowly scanned the pathway behind and to the sides. The gate leading into Dicca lay a good quarter-mile away. To either side was grassy meadow leading to low knolls concealing any more of the park from her.

The tiger leaped.

Inyx ducked directly to one side. Once committed, the cat had to finish its attack. Four-legged animals lack sideways mobility. Inyx whipped out her sword in the time it took the tiger to land, recover, and turn to face her again. It bared yellowed teeth in silent rage now. No voice, just raw hatred. Eyes burning red, it again pounced.

This time Inyx didn't try to fully avoid the attack. She dropped to one knee and braced the sword's pommel against the ground, blade pointing up. Heavy paws raked at her even as the cat's body impaled itself on the sword.

Inyx fell back, stunned, not by the force of the impact

but by the lack of it. She'd been prepared to twist her sword and pull it sideways to keep it from being trapped under the massive cat.

Nothing of the sort had happened.

Her sword remained where it was, pommel in ground. The tiger had vanished as if it had never existed.

"But I saw it!" she protested to empty air. "I did!"

Scooping up her sword, she spun in every direction, frantically looking for the tiger. It wasn't to be seen. Calming herself through great effort, Inyx sniffed the air. No feline spoor. Dropping to the ground to examine the soft dirt failed to reveal any evidence of a heavy predator. Only her own boot soles marked the earth.

Clanking filled the air. She turned, sword in hand. A mechanical parody of a human trooped over a knoll toward her.

"Good lady, do you require assistance? I saw your fluttercraft crash."

"Who are you?"

"Knokno, the park attendant. Are you injured?"

"My fluttercraft was stolen."

The mechanical's glass eyes flashed on and off in amber-colored mock disbelief.

"In *my* park? Such a thing cannot happen. Was the thief a woman, about your height, perhaps twice as heavy, dressed rather shabbily and caked with filth?"

"You know her, then."

"Old Toni we call her. The Lord alone knows what her real name is. Yes, she's a thief. I try to keep her away, but it is such a difficult job. Once my back is turned . . ." Knokno made a human shrugging gesture, cogwheel-driven shoulders moving in the proper directions.

"I just want out of here."

"Why not stay and enjoy the park? I assure you that you will have a fun-filled, rewarding time. You look distraught and needy of entertainment. What is your pleasure, good lady?"

"Getting away from them," she said in a low voice. Four grey-clad soldiers marched down the path. Knokno canted his head to one side and peered at them.

"Ah, yes, they are real. Getting away from them, as you put it, is much more difficult than escaping from my creations, even my most intricate ones."

Inyx began walking, the mechanical following her. They topped the knoll and left the soldiers behind. They hadn't taken any notice of her, for which Inyx was grateful. The fluttercraft trip, the dealings with the trapped demon, the craft's theft, and the tiger attack had left her a little on the confused side. She'd been too long in the white limbo between worlds to be in top fighting form.

"What do you mean, 'your creations'?"

"Why, most everything inside the park boundaries is mine," proudly said the mechanical.

"Even the tiger? One attacked me. A huge cat. Never seen one larger."

"Attacked you? A tiger? Oh, my. I intended him for Constable Luffkin."

"You want to get rid of this Constable Luffkin?"

"No, no, good lady. The Constable *asked* for a tiger image. He fancies himself some sort of big-game hunter. Tigers are extinct in all but the southernmost province of Torr."

"Tiger image?"

"It's not real. Nothing in the park is real. This is an amusement park, good lady. A real tiger is *dangerous*."

"I know," Inyx said. She heaved a sigh and tried to compose her thoughts. The trapped demon had known and hadn't told her this was an amusement park. It had been interested only in escaping its work assignment powering the fluttercraft. Her eyes tipped skyward, seeking the craft. Only tiny dots high above were visible. They moved much too fast for fluttercraft.

"You have encountered a real tiger?" asked the mechanical. The eagerness in his voice was almost comical. "Tell me about it. Did my image match the real thing? Should I have added a few more touches? Like smell? What do real tigers smell like?"

"It was a great image. Had me fooled completely." The woman remembered her initial fright. Even after the first attack she had continued believing in the reality of the tiger. "Would it have hurt me if its attack had connected?"

"Oh, well," hedged the mechanical.

"It would have killed me, wouldn't it?"

"Sometimes I go a bit overboard with my images. That one was a specialty item, and I put ever so much work into it. It might have been a *bit* too much on the substantial side." Knokno averted his glassy eyes and looked at the ground.

"So the images and the real thing might as well be one and the same."

"I do very good work. About the best in Dicca."

"No argument from me on that point," she admitted. "Tell me a little about Dicca and maybe I'll forget to report that to your superior." Inyx wasn't even sure the mechanical had a superior. This world grew increasingly complex. Flying craft, demons, soldiers who weren't even armed with swords, images more deadly than the real thing, talking clockwork mockeries of humans—it all struck her as bizarre.

"What do you want to know?"

"I'm from out of town."

"Oh, one of the outlanders come in to take part in the election." Knokno gave the impression of relaxing visibly, though how a creature of steel limbs and glass joints relaxed wasn't too clear to Inyx. He had somehow placed Inyx into a convenient niche in his ordering of things around him and was content. She didn't want to shake him from this complacency, so she agreed with his appraisal. "Well," he said, "the elections are truly important. The Lord of the Twistings has promised the fairest elections ever."

"But . . . ?" she probed.

"But the grey-clads are doing so much to discourage opposition to the current Lord of the Twistings. I understand some of those most likely to stand against the Lord have . . . vanished."

"Under mysterious circumstances," she finished.

"You might say that."

In the distance came a trumpeting noise. Inyx turned to see a long, slender neck rising above a foggy shore along a small lake. The snakelike neck whipped this way and that until deciding on a proper direction of travel. The gargantuan body following the tiny head and long neck dwarfed the largest of animals Inyx had ever seen.

"Another nice creation. Our natural history section found bones in a tar pit matching such a beast. The purple skin is my idea." Knokno proudly pointed toward the behemoth.

"About the election," Inyx said weakly, her eyes never leaving the monster now sloshing through the murky waters of the still lake.

"About the only firm opposition is Jonrod the Flash. And everyone knows what *he's* like."

The lake monster trumpeted again. An answering challenge rumbled upward to where Inyx sat.

"Knokno, show me out of the park, will you? I've got to find suitable lodging before it gets too dark. I don't know my way around town very well."

"Being from the outlands, that is understandable." The mechanical rose and helped Inyx to her feet. She didn't want to chance even a fraction of a second with the monster noisily sucking up green water from the middle of the lake. Nervous, she kept glancing toward the stagnant pond. "Just be sure to avoid Luister len-Larrotti over on Lossal Boulevard."

Distracted, she only partially heard.

"What? Right. Lossal Boulevard. Look, can we leave now? I wouldn't want to be late." Inyx saw a second monster approaching. The two giant creatures faced off, ready for combat. As large as they were, either could step on her and never even notice the lump under its foot. Before she dropped out of sight behind a hill, the two long-necked creatures were savagely battering one another, knifelike teeth slashing and sending out a rain of imaginary blood.

Inyx could do without imaginary death.

"Here's the gateway into the city. Remember what I said," cautioned the mechanical.

"Lossal Boulevard."

"Right. Luister len-Larrotti."

"Got it. And thanks, Knokno."

"Just don't mention it." Lower, the mechanical added, "To my boss. Won't do having humans killed in the park. He'd scrap me for sure." All the way back into the park, the mechanical mumbled. Inyx heaved a sigh of relief when she saw Dicca proper.

Streets. Paved. People wandering along. Campaign posters plastered on every wall. Hustle. This was her world, not that of illusion inside the park.

Whistling to herself, she set off to find Lossal Boulevard, where Knokno had said she could find lodging.

Inyx tried to remember the name Knokno had given her. She'd been distracted at the time and couldn't—quite— remember. Still, she'd found Lossal Boulevard easily enough. It turned out to be a major arterial cutting through the heart of Dicca. Lined with shops, she found enough to eat. The vendors didn't even give her strange gold pieces a second look as they exchanged their wares for them. Inyx felt she was being cheated and overcharged, but she said nothing.

Raising a fuss might be the stupidest thing she could do. Everywhere throughout the city were Claybore's soldiers. Their presence kept even the most boisterous quiet. Many of the citizens around her grumbled, but none came out and spoke against the grey soldiers. Whether from fear or approval, it was hard to say.

Inyx wandered, looking at the wares offered in the many stores along Lossal. The street turned increasingly dingy and more people lounged in doorways, eyeing her in suspicion and lust. She straightened her shoulders and made sure her sword was near at hand. Never had she turned and run because of being in a strange, unfriendly portion of a town. Inyx sought out such places; they made her travels along the Cenotaph Road more interesting, if more dangerous.

"Luister Something-or-other," she said to one man leaning bonelessly in a doorway. "Do you know of him?"

"Luister's a common-enough name," came the answer. The man picked his teeth with a slender steel spike as his eyes took in Inyx's form. He didn't miss a thing, not the trim waist, the slender legs, the womanly swell of her breasts, the piercing blue eyes, or the lustrous black hair. She almost laughed in the man's face when she saw his look. Inyx had seen it before, and in men with a much better chance of doing what the man mentally considered.

The amused expression on her face made him stiffen.

"Luister len-Larrotti's down the spittin' street."

"Thank you."

"You're welcome, bitch. You two deserve one another."

She turned and glanced back over her shoulder. The man wilted, seeming to collapse in onto himself. He turned and walked off hurriedly. Inyx wondered at the parting curse. It made no sense to her. She continued on, the fatigue of her plight finally catching up with her. When she saw a small sign dangling out from a stone facade, she sighed in relief. *Luister len-Larrotti, Fine Rooms*, it read.

She knocked. A small peephole opened. A rheumy eye peered forth, studying her.

"What do you want?" came the question, muffled so much by the thick wooden door that Inyx couldn't tell if the voice belonged to male or female.

"A room. A friend recommended your boarding house."
Inyx began to wonder why Knokno had bothered mentioning this place.

"You wish to stay?"

"What a ridiculous question. I just said I did." She stamped her foot and took a deep breath. She quickly lost patience with this interrogation. The eye again studied her.

Then the door opened. In the shadows stood an elderly woman, shawl pulled over her shoulders. The old woman gestured Inyx inside. The door closed and bolted behind them, she finally spoke.

"Not often I see the likes of you. You're a young'un, aren't you?" The old woman reached out and pinched Inyx's behind. If a man had done that, his hand would have been severed from his wrist in an instant. Inyx didn't know quite how to respond to a woman old enough to be her grandmother.

"I'm from the outlands. In for the election," she lied. The old woman bobbed a greying head in acknowledgment. "I only need the room until the election's over."

"Can always put up a fine lass like you for a week." Inyx mentally filed the information away. About a week until the election for Lord of the Twistings.

"How much?"

"Don't worry yourself over that none. Come in, sit, enjoy some of my fine herb tea. Don't see many visitors here. Not recently, not ones as pretty as you. Some muffins? Made 'em myself."

The room made Inyx force back a tear in her eye. It so closely matched her mother's parlor that she felt transported across worlds, backward in time. But all this was gone on her home world. Gone forever, along with her mother, brothers, and husband.

"Eat. Sit and eat. And drink the tea. Brewed it myself. Good, or so's everyone tells me."

"Hmm, it is good," said Inyx, surprised. The tea daintily tingled on her tastebuds, exciting a cinnamon taste that mingled subtly with peppermint—or perhaps lemons. She failed to pinpoint the exact taste. Trying the muffins, she found them equally good. They satisfied her growing hunger better than any of the meat and cheese she'd purchased from the vendors along Lossal.

"So seldom we sees fine ones like you," repeated the old woman. She sank into a chair across from Inyx. "Tell me about yourself. In for the election, but who's tending the farm with you here?"

"No one," Inyx said. "Fact is, I'm a traveller from much further away than the outlands."

"The Cenotaph Road?"

"You know of the Road, then." Somehow, this made her relax even more. This kindly old woman already knew of interworld travel. "I'm trying to find friends of mine."

"Your party has become separated?" came the sharp question. Inyx relaxed even more. Here was someone to care for her, someone who knew all her woes.

"They follow, but I don't know how long they'll be. The grey-clad soldiers chased me off, away from the cenotaph." Inyx found herself confiding in the woman. She told of the demon, the fluttercraft flight into Dicca, the deadly illusions she'd confronted in the park. And she told even more, things that had remained buried under the brittle crust of hurtful memory for too long.

"My husband Reinhardt," she heard herself saying, "died almost three years ago. It's hard figuring out exactly when because of time differences between worlds. It must have been three years; it seems to me like an eternity."

"You loved him much."

"Yes." Inyx sighed, picturing tall, dashing Reinhardt in her mind. The dark hair and white smile, the three parallel pink scars on his right cheek where the winter bear had slashed him, the quickness of his movements—she saw it all again. And it hurt.

"Along the Cenotaph Road, no one dies," came the old woman's soft words.

"Reinhardt is dead. I buried him with my own hands. It was one of those damned foolish things that should never have happened. He and my brother Patrin got involved in politics, an election . . ."

"Like the one for Lord of the Twistings?"

"Different. The election was for nothing of any consequence, but others didn't consider it such. Others wearing grey uniforms."

"The soldiers killed him?"

"They ambushed him. Patrin lived long enough to tell me where. I found Reinhardt. He died in my arms. And then I tracked down and killed every single one of those murdering bastards. I killed them, slowly, as slowly as I could." She felt the horror and terror and anguish welling inside her. Inyx relived Reinhardt's death, those of the murdering soldiers sent by Claybore to subjugate her world. "Then I walked the Cenotaph Road. There was nothing of importance left for me on my own world. Nothing."

"The soldiers' deaths might rekindle Reinhardt's flame. Somewhere along the Road, he again lives."

"I don't believe that. I . . ." Inyx stopped, the words choking her. The old woman grew in stature, shoulders widening, shape changing in eye-confusing shifts until a tall, dark man with perfect white teeth stood before Inyx.

"Reinhardt!" she cried.

"My dearest Inyx. It's been so long. Too long. My love!"

Strong arms held her in the embrace she had hungered for over three long, lonely years. She buried her face in his chest and unashamedly cried.

"Reinhardt, where have you been? How could you have let me think you were dead all this time?"

"No questions, my dearest. Not now. Not until after a proper homecoming." His strong, blunt fingers worked at the ties on her tunic. Inyx felt a pang of—what? Confusion tried to turn her inside out. Then the remembered feel of Reinhardt's hands on her breasts drove away all uncertainty.

She crushed her body to his, kissed him hungrily, felt him respond. Almost frantic now, the passionate lovers worked to get free of unwanted clothing.

On the floor, their bodies merged into one surging, striving unity. Inyx felt the heavy body weighing her down in familiar ways, the pressures inside, the heavy breathing in her ear. She stared at the ceiling, dread welling up inside again. Something was wrong, something still niggled at the fringes of her mind. Then she forgot all about it, gasping, crying, rejoicing.

"Reinhardt!" she cried. "Oh, Reinhardt, yes!"

CHAPTER FIVE

"Oh, woe, why must I be such a weakling? A craven, that is all I am," lamented Krek. The giant spider walked in the center of a ring of twelve soldiers. They eyed him with a combination of fear and awe. Lan Martak guessed that creatures the size of Krek didn't exist on this world—or if they did, they weren't inclined to talk and berate themselves.

"It wasn't anyone's fault, Krek," he said. "The howler spotted us and guided the soldiers in."

"I could have fought. Oh, the horror of it. Krek-k'with-kritlike, Webmaster of the Egrii Mountains, has fallen on such hard times. And all because I am so cowardly." Lan said nothing. He'd seen his friend in moods like this before. Absolutely nothing but time got him out of them. "Who am I to even breathe the name of Webmaster? I, who have shamed myself in the eyes of all my hatchlings? Lovely little Klawn knows me for what I am. A coward. I can never again hold up my head."

Lan involuntarily shivered when Krek mentioned his mate's name. Krek was enormous; "lovely little Klawn" was even larger. She and the giant spider had mated, then Krek had left the web before being ritualistically eaten by her. Choosing the Cenotaph Road over being devoured seemed to Lan a reasonable choice. For Krek, it went against all his race's mores and genetically inbred behavior patterns. Somewhere, perhaps even on this world, Klawn followed along the Road, still seeking her mate to finalize the nuptials. Lan didn't want to share even the same continent with that love-crazed female.

"And if that were not enough, in the Suzerain's care I slaughtered helpless innocents. With these I slaughtered them!" Krek clashed together his mandibles. The noise echoed across still forests. The soldiers guarding him jumped in alarm, their hands reaching automatically for the tubes they carried at their sides.

Lan frowned when he saw this reaction. He'd guessed those were weapons of some sort. But what type? While his magic sense required much more honing, it didn't give the slightest twinge when he studied those tubes. Rather than magic, they utilized mechanical principles, much like the robotic servants encountered on the world he and Krek had just vacated.

He had no "feel" of magic being used by any of the men. If anything, they relied too heavily on the ordinary world around them. His ears turned toward the leader as he grumbled about having to walk.

"If she hadn't stolen our fluttercraft . . ." was all Lan overheard. But hope surged. *She* the captain had said. Lan had no idea what a fluttercraft was, but the *she* had to mean Inyx.

It had to!

"You mean we're walking because Inyx robbed you?" Lan called out to the officer in charge.

"What? You know her?" came the immediate question.

"Captain, the spider," complained one of the guards. Krek had dropped into a forlorn lump in the middle of the road, refusing to go on. He wept, tears staining the areas under his dun-colored eyes and eventually dripping onto

his furred legs and matting them. This, for the spider, was
the ultimate in degradation.

"Halt!" ordered the leader. To Lan he said, "Get the
bug moving again or we move it for you."

"He's not a bug," said Lan, indignant. "He's an intelligent being. More so than you, I can see."

The captain pulled forth his tube and aimed it directly at
Lan's midsection. Not knowing what the device did made
Lan more uneasy than if he'd possessed intimate knowledge of its workings. On his home world those entrusted
with law enforcement sometimes used wheel lock pistols.
Those were cranky, delicate, and not very accurate, yet
they killed at a considerable range. While he didn't see
any clockwork firing mechanism on the sides of the soldiers'
weapons, he guessed they, too, had the ability to kill at a
distance.

When Lan didn't properly respond, the soldier slowly
swung his cylinder in an arc until it pointed at Krek. At the
last possible moment before pressing an inset firing button,
the captain lowered his aim. A finger-thick beam of intense light speared forth and vaporized the dirt just under
Krek's back legs.

Startled and frightened, the spider leaped straight up
into the air. For an instant, Lan stood open-mouthed and
gaping, just like the soldiers. Krek had become airborne,
his eight coppery legs spread from his body like a furry
pinwheel. He landed with a heavy thud, whirling to face
the captain of the guard.

"Never do that to me again," the spider raged. "You
could have set my fur on fire!"

"I'll do more than that if you don't get your bulky
carcass moving. It's a long way into Dicca. Silvain'll have
my head on a spike for taking so long, as it is."

"Silvain?" asked Lan quietly.

"Shut up and get moving." This time the imperious
gesture with the tube got both Lan and Krek trotting along.

Close enough to carry on a low-whispered conversation,

Lan asked his friend, "Have you ever seen the likes of their weapons before?"

"Never," said Krek. "Nor have I heard of worlds where such are possible. Do they hide little fire elementals in each weapon? It seems a magical chore hardly worth accomplishing."

"It's not done magically," Lan said. "I don't 'see' any spells being used."

"One little book and the boy thinks he is a master sorcerer," scoffed Krek.

"I know what I know," said Lan defensively. "However they produce the light beam, it's not done magically. This world is more advanced technologically, but I think I can get around that with a few well-chosen spells."

"Make me invisible first."

"I don't know how to do that," said Lan. "I don't even know if it's possible."

"I don't even know if your plan is possible," countered Krek.

They walked in silence for another mile before Lan calmed down enough to speak again.

"Remember how Claybore's death beams bent around me? I think I can control that spell now. Before, it came to me on a subconscious level. I've been working on drawing it to the surface of my mind. I know it will work."

"You try it first. But before you do, what was that I heard about Inyx? You mentioned her name to the grey-clad soldier captain."

"He said a woman had stolen their fluttercraft, whatever that is. Some form of transportation, apparently. I didn't get any good idea of when this happened, but it explains why they don't have her as a prisoner."

"Like they do us."

"Krek, we can escape whenever we want. I'm playing along to get information."

"About Dicca, the capital city where the Lord of the Twistings rules supreme?" said the spider in an arrogant tone. "I know all. I hear so much you do not. They take us to Alberto Silvain, Claybore's commandant on this planet. Or so I surmise. Silvain is the military governor who ordered these miserable wights out to intercept us. I assume he learned of the cenotaph through Claybore's magics. Silvain is occupied with elections in Dicca. These odd sorting processes you humans use are rigged in this instance, with the Lord of the Twistings the shoo-in favorite because of bought votes and Claybore's influence."

"What else have you overheard?" asked Lan.

"Nothing."

Lan shook his head. The spider managed to be vexing, even when he didn't try very hard. Still, with the information they now shared, Lan saw little reason to remain in the custody of the soldiers. They weren't of the highest caliber. They jumped at their own shadows and knew nothing of woodlore. Claybore's usual tactic was to bring in a few key officers, then recruit locals for his army. He paid well and offered quick promotions. Such things appealed to the lower types. All the while, they were being exploited and used for interworld conquest.

Lan doubted any of these men realized Claybore's designs extended across dozens, maybe hundreds of worlds. Alberto Silvain knew, just as Kiska k'Adesina had a world back and Lyk Surepta on Lan's home world. A privileged, powerful few leading the ignorant, greedy many.

It was a conquest plan that worked all too well.

When the howler screamed across the sky, Lan Martak acted.

The soldiers stopped to gawk. They were natives of this world, but the sight of a howler still meant a special treat for them. Lan jerked to one side, kicked at a kneecap, and felt it crunch, then grabbed. He had regained his sword and dagger. Against the death tubes, these meant little, but he had magic on his side.

"Die, you spitting scum," came the captain's curse.

Lan's eyes glazed over as he summoned up all the inner

power resting inside him. He remembered the nightmare battles with Claybore when the sorcerer's skull cast forth the twin ruby death beams. The ruby shafts had parted, bent around Lan's body. He mentally clutched at that spell now and moulded it for his own use.

The captain fired.

The lambent energy deflected from Lan at the last possible instant. The spell had worked. Barely.

The confusion on the captain's face told Lan all he needed to know. The weapon had been given to the man with instructions and praise for its invincibility. Now that it had failed, he had no idea what to try next. Lan didn't give him time to decide. Two quick steps and a swing of the sword sent hand and cylinder rolling.

Clutching his spurting stump, the man screamed in shock and fell into a shallow irrigation ditch, slowly filling the dirt channel with his life's blood.

"Run!" cried Lan. Many of the soldiers took it as a command—or a convenient reason for leaving the scene of such carnage. Only a few hesitated. One raised his own weapon.

Lan's mind felt as if it had slipped onto greased glass. He struggled to bring up the proper spells. His concentration had lapsed upon seeing the captain die. There wasn't any way he could re-form his protective spell in time to be effective. He brought up the blade of his sword in a reflex action.

The death beam squarely struck his shiny sword and reflected away harmlessly. The attacking grey-clad blinked, then aimed again. Lan reflected the beam directly back into the man's body. He died, his belly a smoky ruin.

"He killed Molok with his own pistol," cried one of the two remaining soldiers.

"AAARRGHHH!" roared Krek, rising up on his eight long legs. His mandibles crashed together like scythes. The soldiers saw death advancing on them, turned, and ran.

"I say," said Krek, "I did not think I was *that* frightening. I am relieved, though, to have avoided an ugly confrontation. Ever since my days in the arena killing those poor boys and girls, it is difficult for me to get into the spirit."

"You were forced to kill then, Krek. Now you fight to protect yourself—and your friends. Thanks. You certainly saved me."

"That was an interesting trick with your sword. How did you know it would work?"

"Seemed likely," Lan said hurriedly. He didn't want to let his friend know it was purely accidental that he'd even tried it. "Let's get moving for Dicca. Unless I miss my guess, Inyx is waiting for us there."

"Probably nice and dry, well fed, and dangling in a wonderful web," said the spider, head bobbing in agreement.

CHAPTER SIX

Inyx stirred, moaned softly, and reached out. Her arms felt soft, pliant, flabby flesh when she should have found nothing but firmly toned muscle. Vivid blue eyes fluttering open, she stared at the man in bed next to her.

"Reinhardt?" she asked, her voice still husky and her eyes gummy with sleep.

"Yes, my love."

The softness under her fingers never changed, but the shape altered subtly. She blinked harder and stared. Reinhardt smiled at her, his perfect, even teeth shining whitely in the soft light filtering through the window. The four parallel scars on his cheek glowed.

Four?

Inyx sat up.

"There should be three scars," she said.

"What's this, my dearest?"

The woman looked harder. There *were* three. She'd been mistaken.

Or had she?

"Where have you been for these years, Reinhardt? Why did you make me suffer? How did you . . . ?"

"Shush, my darling," he said, pressing a finger to her lips. "This is not the time for talk. It's a time for rediscovery, for love."

She felt his hands moving slowly over her naked body. Old responses rose within her, responses she cherished and had denied herself since he'd died—gone away. She sighed and sank back to the bed. But Inyx worried. Something wasn't right. The scars. Three or four? The flesh under her fingers, the weight pressing her into the mattress, the *feel* of the way Reinhardt made love to her.

Then her passions consumed all doubt and she cried out in joy. She'd found her beloved Reinhardt and would never let him go. Never!

Inyx awoke in midafternoon. She rose from the bed and found her clothing. Silently, she put on tunic and trousers, noting that her weapons were gone. Living with them as her constant companions for all these years made her feel more naked without them than when she wore no clothes. She looked around the small room, looking for a spot where Reinhardt might have laid them.

The room was dingy in the extreme. White and blue striped roaches frolicked along the rotting floorboards, darting in and out and mocking her attempts to step on them. The light coming through the window revealed a coating of dust on the pane thick enough to give a brown tint to everything in the room; one small pane had been broken and not replaced. Curtains hanging in tatters added little class to the place. Inyx sat heavily on the bed, heard the springs protesting mightily. The bedclothes were grey—once they'd been white. The pillows were lumpy. The mattress ticking poked through in heavy knots. The head-board had been sloppily painted years ago and was now peeled and chipped.

"At least that matches the walls," she said glumly. But, in spite of the sordid surroundings, she had to feel a warm inner glow.

Reinhardt.

She'd thought him dead all those years, killed by the grey-clad soldiers as they attempted to take over her home world. The woman flopped back on the rickety bed and stretched like a cat in the warm summer sun. She felt good all over, for the first time in recent memory.

Reinhardt!

Footsteps sounded outside. From the tentative quality of the tread, she guessed someone tried to walk softly and keep the floorboards from creaking. They failed. In this boarding house, only faith kept the roof from falling down or the floors from collapsing.

"Reinhardt, is that you?" she called out.

"Yes, my dearest." Inyx felt a moment of giddy shifting, then the door opened. Her husband stood there, a tray of food in hand. "I brought you lunch. You've slept most of the day."

"I . . . I'm still a little sleepy," she confessed. "But it was so good being with you last night. It's so good being with you now."

He batted away her teasing fingers.

"Not now. I have work to do. You eat."

"But Reinhardt, let me help. I can . . ."

"Eat." The word came out sharp, brittle, a definite command. Inyx had been walking the Cenotaph Road for three years and had learned to rebel against such orders. In spite of the fact that this was her beloved husband Reinhardt, she only pretended to eat the food. A little sleight of hand slipped most of it under the bed for the gourmet feasting of the roaches. It'd hardly be noticed with all the other debris there, she guessed.

"I'm finished," she said. Reinhardt stirred from across the room and looked at the plate. He nodded curtly, turned, and left.

"Wait!" she cried. By the time she reached the door, it had been locked from the outside. "Reinhardt, why are you doing this to me?'' Inyx thought she heard a cruel laugh, but wasn't certain.

Did Reinhardt have three or four scars on his cheek?

She slept fitfully, awakening from a nightmare combining tigers, Reinhardt, and grey soldiers on one side against her, Lan and Krek on the other defending her. Inyx wiped away sweat and took a deep breath to regain her composure. It was an odd dream. Reinhardt should have been aiding her, not opposing her.

Voices drifted up through the flooring. She shook off a slight dizziness and got out of bed, pressing her ear to the wood planking. What Inyx heard turned her cold inside.

". . . best I've ever seen. Great legs, too,'' bragged a man. She recognized the voice only after difficult concentration. It sounded much like Reinhardt. "I'll keep her up in the room till after the election. I can make at least a score a tumble with her and have the men lined up around the block waiting their turn. The women, too! She's a fine one, she is.''

"Really, Luister, I couldn't care less about your crude sexual exploitations. You owe me eighty score interest on the loan. My superiors are very upset over the lack of payment.'' The voice turned icy with menace. "If you don't pay a hundred score by the end of the week, we shall have to take over your Fine Rooms.''

Inyx frowned. The way the man said "Fine Rooms'' sounded as if it meant something more than a description of a boarding room. The contempt carried in his tones were those a churchgoer reserves for "whorehouse.'' She slipped fingernails between the boards and pulled. Pain shot up her arms, but she had to see. After a wooden protest, the flooring parted enough for her to look into the room below.

A man dressed in a black suit over a frilly white shirt stood by the door. He gave the grossly overweight man seated in a chair a look cold enough to freeze fire.

"One hundred score by the end of the week. You will not like the alternative, len-Larrotti. I promise you that."

"Odissan, you bore me. I tell you that everything's going to be fine now that I've got some high-class talent to sell."

"Maybe you will actually have a fine room," said Odissan. "It doesn't matter. Good day to you."

The bloated frog of a man seated just at the edge of Inyx's field of view made an obscene gesture at the departing man's back. He rocked back in the chair and drummed stubby fingers on the battered chair arms. Inyx felt a wave of polar clarity wash through her brain. Everything fit into place.

This was Reinhardt. Or rather this gross blimp of a man had made her believe he was her husband. Reinhardt had died three years ago. Somehow she had been duped into thinking he still lived. The herb tea, the muffins, something had drugged her. Her thoughts were disturbed by someone knocking on the door below. She watched as Luister len-Larrotti rose and waddled forth.

As he walked, his form shifted, flowed. He became an old woman—the same one who had greeted her yesterday.

"Come in, my boy," cackled the old woman—Luister len-Larrotti. He ushered into the parlor an adolescent male, obviously nervous. "What can I do for you? Some herb tea? The muffins are superb."

"I . . . I want a Fine Room."

"Such a youth, so big and muscular. A real brawler. You want only the best, I'd wager."

"Yes," he said, head bobbing as if it were on springs. "The best."

"How much do you have?" The bite of greed made Inyx recoil. How the youth missed it was beyond her. Yet she couldn't be too critical. She had entirely missed the illusion directed at her the day before.

She shuddered. Even worse, she had accepted the illusion of her dead husband as real. She'd wanted it to be true, and Luister len-Larrotti had played on that weakness, changing his form to match her every need. He was nothing more than a human chameleon, moulding himself to mood as well as physical surroundings.

"So much? Two score? You get the best."

"My m-mother," the youth stammered.

"She knows of your . . . love," said len-Larrotti. "And she is anxiously awaiting you upstairs. Come, I'll show you the way to the best Fine Room in the house."

Inyx listened to the footsteps outside her door. One was heavy, confident. The other set came hesitantly. A hand rested on the handle. Inyx stood, fists tensed at her side. She'd fight her way out, if she could.

But magics permeated the room, gripping her, confusing her, turning her inside out. She felt her knees go weak and all resolve drain away. When the door opened, her Reinhardt stood there. How could she fight the man she loved?

"My dearest," he said, his voice ringing forth in the baritone she knew and loved so well. He came to her, undressed her, made love to her. Inyx shivered after he left.

Faint words drifted up through the floorboards.

". . . Luister, you were right. She was worth it. You run the best Fine Room in all of Dicca."

"Come back soon."

Inyx rolled over in the shabby bed and began to cry.

"It will be an exciting new venture for us, my dear," Reinhardt told her. She carefully hid away the food he'd given her and artfully poured the herb tea behind the bed. Inyx faced slow starvation, but in the past two days she'd learned that her first suspicions had been correct: the food was drugged. By not eating, she maintained some semblance of her former self.

But all resistance faded whenever Reinhardt came into the room. She knew now that her husband was dead, that this was Luister len-Larrotti hiding behind illusion. She knew it intellectually; emotions presented another facet Inyx couldn't cope with. She *wanted* Reinhardt to live, to breathe, to hold her in his arms and love her. She *wanted* that with all her heart and soul.

Luister len-Larrotti used it against her.

"There will be customers coming to the diorama, paying good coin to see you in your full glorious beauty. This will be the finest exhibit of its kind in all of Dicca."

She stared at Reinhardt—len-Larrotti. Four scars on the cheek. Even as she doubted, the illusion changed.

"Why are you doing this?"

A sly look totally unlike Reinhardt came and went on the handsome face of the man confronting her. He smiled, and the smile took on evil qualities.

"My dearest, I want all of Dicca to share what I possess."

Inyx repressed a shudder. Since coming to this place len-Larrotti had paraded men and women through this tiny room. All had made love to her—raped her. And in each she had seen Reinhardt. What had they seen? Len-Larrotti's magics provided illusion, for a price. He grew rich off others' obsessions and guilty desires.

"What of the Lord of the Twistings?" she asked.

"You jump from topic to topic, my dear. What of the Lord? The election is soon, only days away."

"What does he do?"

"He rules, of course. What an odd question. Now, come with me. I will show you the new quarters I have prepared for you. Fine ones they are, too."

"Fine magics?" she asked, her temper flaring. Inyx realized that len-Larrotti stiffened, although the Reinhardt facade he adopted barely moved.

"You will like the new quarters," he said, voice flat and cold.

She allowed him to lead her away from the room where she'd been imprisoned. The new one hardly suited Inyx more. It had a bed in it, no better than the one she left behind. There was also a large window facing Lossal Boulevard. She went to the window and touched fingertips against it. Pressing her slightly feverish cheek onto coolness brought a moment of mental clarity.

The bloated slug of a man holding her magically bound smiled ominously. She'd be used in even more degrading fashion. And she'd do it. Fight as she would, the hold of Reinhardt's memory was stronger than her will.

"The first customers come. Enjoy, dearest, enjoy, and they will also!" Laughter filled the room in which she was on display, like an animal in a zoo cage.

"Show me what they see," she said in a listless voice. For another two days she'd been locked up in len-Larrotti's picture-window room, her every intimate moment on display to anyone passing by outside. She'd lost track of the men who'd used her in that time. She fought but it did no good. They all were Reinhardt. All.

"You know there is only me," said the man. She had learned to distinguish between Luister len-Larrotti as Reinhardt and his whoremongering customers, who also appeared to her as her dead husband.

"Show me."

Out of cruelty, he did. A small group gathered outside the window to peer in at her. She closed her eyes and then opened them. The man nearest saw her in a tawdry corset, net stockings, and high spiked heels. The man next to him saw her as a plain country girl, barely fourteen—a lost love. The one in the back of the crowd viewed her magically altered appearance as male, burly, rough. Inyx began to cry softly.

Out of stark hunger, she had been eating small bits of the food len-Larrotti brought her. The effects of the drug wore off quickly enough because little entered her bloodstream. But the paucity of food also made her progressively weaker and less able to resist the drug's insidious shape-changing effects. Immediately after she ate, the man would come to her while the image of Reinhardt burned brightly in her mind.

Once, when len-Larrotti lay beside her, sated, she had whispered, "Why do you use me? Why me?"

"Reality is hard enough to change," he muttered, more asleep than awake. "You require very little altering in illusion. You are so close to perfection, only small magics give them what they want."

She watched heavy eyelids lower. Reinhardt. Inyx had reached out to caress. Her fingers found flabby throat, squeezed down on multiple chins. Reinhardt. She killed her own husband. The woman hesitated, then her resolve hardened. But it came too late. A convulsive jerk had allowed the man to break her grip and rise. She sat in bed, staring in dumb horror at her hands, as if they had betrayed her.

Luister len-Larrotti left, only to admit a steady string of patrons, all of whom looked exactly like lost Reinhardt. The magics strengthened against her, and she never again had the opportunity to kill her tormentor.

Inyx sat and watched, sometimes wondering what those outside saw, other times not caring. For all the traffic, not once did a grey-clad soldier stop and gawk. Their rules must prohibit use of Fine Rooms, she guessed. Whether that was a mercy or not, she couldn't say. It might be better having them discover her and then execute her rather than continue providing cheap sexual thrills for len-Larrotti and his customers.

Inyx sat and concentrated, forcing her will down, ever down inside her. The point where she concentrated burned with fiery need. She fanned the flames, nurtured them, let them rise only to deny them. Not enough. She had triumphed over worse. Reinhardt was dead. Luister len-Larrotti imprisoned her. She hated Luister len-Larrotti. Reinhardt had died. Her husband no longer existed, except in her own mind. Inyx worked, moulded, changed, savored, hoarded.

Another man entered the room. Inyx continued to concentrate. She felt len-Larrotti's magics flowing like warm water in a stream, filling the room, threatening to drown her. The woman didn't resist; she went with the flow, moved with it, then began angling to one side. She saw Reinhardt waiting for her by the bed; superimposed over his muscular body she saw a middle-aged, paunchy man. Inyx resisted more. The illusion of Reinhardt wavered.

"I've always wanted to make love to a jungle goddess," the man said. "On your hands and knees. Go sniffing for jungle spoor. Let me stalk you through the jungle."

Inyx did as she was told. Like an animal, she raced around the room, the man joyously pursuing. The illusion faded. As the man caught her, she turned and delivered one silent, swift blow to his neck. He made a small choking noise, then sank onto the bed.

"Oh, Reinhardt," she cooed, in case her captor watched or listened, "you are as much a man as ever. No, more than ever!"

She searched her victim, finding nothing. Cursing softly at this failure, she pulled out a piece of steel supporting the mattress. Using this, she forced the door lock. Inyx felt the flood of magic around her abate slightly. However len-Larrotti focused his spells, that room was the center. The further away from it she got, the less she'd feel the pull.

Stumbling, crying in frustration, knowing the truth and perversely wanting Reinhardt all the more, she reached the door leading to Lossal Boulevard. Trembling hands undid the first bolt. Inyx worked frantically to open the second.

"My dearest Inyx, you aren't leaving me, are you? How could you, after all these years apart? I need you so much."

She looked back over her shoulder. Reinhardt stood there. The look of hurt and betrayal on his face caused her to break down and sob uncontrollably. With her failure to escape came a tiny morsel of success: she again had Reinhardt.

CHAPTER SEVEN

"The grey-clads do not follow us. How odd," said Krek. The spider bounced up and down, craning his almost nonexistent neck back in the direction they'd come. "It has been a goodly four days since I so soundly ran them off. They normally show more persistence. My scare job must have been better than I thought."

With typical arachnid perversity, Krek had neglected to mention Lan's role in routing the soldiers. But the man didn't care. Not being disturbed by Claybore's men, for whatever reason, suited him fine. If Krek wanted to take all the credit for that, let him. And Lan didn't know for sure but that the spider was right. The soldiers had bolted when they'd seen how ferocious an opponent Krek could be.

He touched the cylinder he'd recovered from the slain captain. It aimed easily, just like pointing a wand. The tiny button on the side triggered the death beam. Lan had tried it out on a lightning-blasted tree. A new bolt of fire had reduced the charred tree to smouldering embers. Obviously a more potent weapon than his sword—and faster-acting than his relatively weak fire spells. Lan still felt uneasy with the weapon.

A sword rested solidly in the hand. It swung easily and cut true. And spells conjured up provided a sense of control he didn't get from the death tube.

"Any indication of how much farther it is to Dicca?" he asked the spider.

Krek stopped, dug talons into the dry earth, and stood shivering. Lan waited while his friend "listened" by sensing faint vibrations in the ground. Krek finally straightened and shook his head.

"Nothing. But then, we see very little ground traffic. Aerial forms of travel abound." Even as he spoke, a V-shaped flight of howlers rocketed across the sky. Crossing from horizon to horizon took only seconds.

"Most of those things," Lan said with distaste, indicating the howlers, "are too small for more than two people. They must have larger versions or the roads would be packed with travellers. The more advanced a world, the more it requires communication of both goods and ideas."

"How profound," said Krek. Lan Martak glanced sharply at him, wondering if the spider intended that as sarcasm. He couldn't tell. "Inyx travelling in one of the fluttercraft puts her days ahead of us."

"We're making good time. Did you detect any others along this road?"

"Something massive rumbles in this direction."

"Might be a troop carrier. Let's get off the road and wait for a while."

"Nonsense, friend Lan Martak," Krek said tartly. "We need to press on. No handful of soldiers can drive us off this fine road."

"You want to face a hundred soldiers capable of setting your legs on fire and never getting within a hundred feet of you?" He tapped the death tube hanging at his belt.

"Well," vacillated the spider, "perhaps it is time to enjoy an afternoon's relaxation."

"It's only about ten in the morning," pointed out Lan, smiling.

"So we are doing it early." The spider hopped to the side of the road and soon found an area where he crouched down and blended into the landscape. From twenty feet away he looked like nothing more than a brown rock with a few wiry roots prying their way up and under. Lan took a post closer to the road. Again he admired Krek's talents for sensing vibration. Living on a web and depending on the proper interpretation of the slightest of twitches had its advantages. A heavy truck rolled along the road.

"No soldiers," he said to Krek. "Looks like produce for the city markets."

The truck rumbled on by. Lan exchanged a quick glance with Krek, then ran after the vehicle. An agile leap brought him into the back to lie amid stacks of fragrant vegetables. He wiped off a long, green stalk of crisp celery and began to eat. The truck lurched sideways, then regained its course. Lan glanced up. The heavy canvas stretched over metal support rods sagged ominously. He smiled to himself. Krek had decided to enjoy the air outside and crouched on the roof.

In a short while, the gentle rolling motion of the truck put Lan to sleep.

"You, what are you doing back there?" demanded the driver. Lan opened one bleary eye and stared at the man. Behind him stretched loading bays, many filled with trucks similar to this one.

"Just catching up on my sleep. Many thanks for the use of your celery." Lan vaulted out and glanced up. Krek perched on the edge of the roof, peering at him.

The driver followed Lan's gaze, saw Krek, then turned back to the human.

"Get out of here."

"My friend, too?" Lan asked, indicating Krek.

"Your friend, too."

This took Lan by surprise. Most people reacted strongly to the sight of an eight-foot-tall spider, especially one preparing to spring on their heads. The driver didn't even cringe.

Krek said amiably, "Thank you for the ride, sir. It was most pleasant."

The driver scowled and pushed Lan aside to begin unloading. Lan nodded to Krek to leave.

Outside the shipping area, Lan said, "Odd he didn't comment on you."

"Yes, it is odd," agreed Krek. "One does not often see a Webmaster this far from the mountains."

Lan shook his head and started walking. After a half-hour he assured himself this was Dicca. It had taken only ten seconds to convince him that an election was imminent. Posters flared, shimmered, and changed form before his eyes, giving animated testimonials for the candidates. He even stopped to listen to one candidate haranguing a small crowd outside his headquarters.

"The current Lord of the Twistings is cheating you, yes, *cheating* you!" the man screamed. "He fails to give you the utter finest. Can he do this?" A small circus of bizarre creatures appeared out of thin air and began to perform.

"Can't see in the back!" called out one of the spectators on the fringe of the crowd.

"You can't see what the Lord gives you, either. But remember this well, Jonrod the Flash will give it to you!"

The tiny animals grew in size, expanding, exploding until the smallest was as large as Krek. The crowd stood and watched the illusory antics while Lan watched the crowd. The man in the rear who had complained about not seeing edged around and talked quietly with Jonrod. Money changed hands. Lan shook his head. The man had been a shill, asking the proper questions on cue. Jonrod hurried back to the front of the crowd just as his images faded.

"That isn't all I can give you. I promise first-rate images every single day. What other candidate goes that far? None, none but Jonrod the Flash."

"Let's go," Lan said to Krek. "Politics bores me. It's always the same, no matter the world. Promise the sky, deliver dirt."

"I find the illusions amusing," said the spider. "Somewhat insubstantial, but amusing."

"You're seeing them differently than I am. I'd swear they were real if I didn't know better. Maybe the truck driver thought you were an illusion and that's why he didn't react."

"An illusion? I, Krek of the Crags? Absurd."

They walked along the street, hardly aware of the difference between reality and image. Lan marvelled that Dicca could survive in this fashion. Jonrod the Flash promised free illusions—in return for voting for him. Others offered fine illusions for sale. One of these stores Lan entered.

"Good sir, how may I aid you?" asked the oily clerk from behind a large desk.

"You sell illusions. I'd like to see what you have in stock."

"In stock?" the clerk parroted, as if Lan had committed a major faux paus. "Illusorium Unlimited *tailors* illusions. We cater exclusively to the . . . best of clientele."

"I understand. I'm able to conjure a bit myself." Lan stepped back and chanted his minor fire spell. Fat blue sparks leaped from finger to finger, then jetted upward in pyrotechnic magnificence. He'd known this spell for many years, having been taught it when he was barely in his teens.

"I see," said the clerk dryly, obviously unimpressed. "That one, the one behind you, that's a more difficult illusion."

Lan turned to see Krek hunkered down behind him. He smiled and said, "That? That's nothing."

"Well, perhaps we can do business. I'm not adverse to trading illusions. I have a market for one such as that. Knokno over in the park is always looking for . . . oddities."

"Oddities?" bellowed Krek. "Who are you calling an oddity?"

Lan motioned the arachnid back.

"Nicely done," said the clerk. "Would you be interested in trading for, say, a forty-foot alligator? No? Here's one that will make you the life of any party."

Lan involuntarily stepped back. A chasm opened in front of him, a large panther pacing at the bottom of the pit.

"Yes, that'd be a million laughs at one of my parties," Lan said. "Really, I'm more interested in one of those." He pointed to a grey-clad soldier marching along the street.

"That's no illusion," said the clerk, his mood shifting. "I wish it were."

"Oh?" Lan felt he skirted the verge of information.

"The Lord of the Twistings says it amuses him allowing them to keep the peace. A spitting nuisance, I say." The man pressed one soft white hand to his lips. "I'm sorry. I shouldn't have used such profanity."

"Which of the candidates for Lord of the Twistings opposes the soldiers?"

"None openly. I understand Jonrod is unwilling to allow them to continue on if he is elected, but then Jonrod is adversely inclined toward anyone supporting the law, if you catch the meaning."

"He and the law are on uneasy terms."

"Exactly." Shifting back into his sales pitch, the clerk asked, "Which do you like, the panther pit or the alligator? I'll trade either for the spider."

"Do you rent?" Lan asked facetiously. The clerk stiffened.

"If you're looking for Fine Rooms, I suggest down south on Lossal, past the markets."

"Fine Rooms?"

"Brothels, low-born."

The clerk's tone left no room for misinterpreting the fact that he desired Lan and his "illusion" out of the store. Lan quickly left, Krek trailing along behind.

"Oddity, indeed," sniffed Krek. "What an odious little man that was."

"It sounds as if Diccans mix magic with their sex," observed Lan. "That was what I took him to mean about 'Fine Rooms.' "

"Imagine comparing me to something like that." The spider sniffed and stalked off, leaving Lan to stare in amazement at a gelatinous cube wobbling down the center of the street. Krek had something there. Being compared with such an amorphous blob would damage one's ego. He hurried to follow the spider.

"This is the damnedest place I've ever seen. I can hardly keep illusion and reality separate."

"It is not that difficult, friend Lan Martak," said the spider. "The illusions waver slightly and always appear slightly translucent. It is quite simple."

"To your eyes, not to mine." He'd found Lossal Boulevard, more out of curiosity than anything else, and seen the signs for Fine Rooms. While the proprietors of most shops selling hard commodities refused to talk openly about the Fine Rooms, Lan learned that all of Lossal was abuzz with a scheme one of them ran.

"A diorama," said one man in low, conspiratorial tones. "Luister len-Larrotti exchanges sex with the woman—or man—of your choice in whatever setting you desire. A most difficult illusion. And he charges for it."

"Where is this len-Larrotti?" Lan asked.

"Oh, good sir, you should avoid a place like that. Luister len-Larrotti will rob you, if he can."

"I'd like to see what's setting up all the furor." Lan honestly did wish to see the window described to him with the wanton in the window performing for those in the streets, but more intimately giving the paying customer a hint of paradise. Anything as talked about in a city bored with common images had to be special.

"He's down the street, south of Mittervault Avenue," the man finally said. "But don't tell anyone I even know where his spittin' Fine Rooms are."

"Fine Rooms are something magical, aren't they?"

"You pay extra. Len-Larrotti must be doing very well. He paid off his loan to Odissan."

"A loan arranger?"

"A thief," the man declared bitterly. Lan didn't have to ask who else owed this Odissan money.

"Thanks for the information." Lan stepped out of the shop, then froze. A half-dozen soldiers trooped down the street. Their captain's quick eyes darted everywhere, studying every pedestrian. Lan was positive he and Krek couldn't elude the woman, even for an instant. He turned north and walked along just fast enough to stay in front of the soldiers.

"They will spot me soon," said Krek. "I cannot mingle as well as you do in human crowds."

"You can't mingle at all, dammit," snapped Lan. "Look for somewhere to hide." He didn't see any place. He felt hot eyes boring into his back. The woman must have seen him. She couldn't have missed him, not with Krek stalking along beside.

There wasn't anywhere to go.

"Good ladies and gentle sirs," came a familiar voice, "I am the best qualified because I am honest. Honest, I say, unlike our current Lord. Jonrod the Flash *shares* his illusions with those who vote for him. Have any of you seen anything this spectacular? It's all yours today, tomorrow, every day until the election—and for a complete term *if* you elect me Lord of the Twistings.''

Two story-tall apparitions bellowed and stalked one another in the street. Lan grabbed one of Krek's legs and pulled him forward. They were caught up at the fringes of the crowd watching Jonrod's illusions battle each other to bloody pulps. As the behemoths sagged, Jonrod refreshed them with new and even more startling creatures. Krek fit right in, hardly noticeable among the truly outrageous creations Jonrod shared with his electorate.

Lan saw the grey-clads advancing, more to watch than act. He moved away from their captain and stood beside Jonrod, leading the cheers and acting as shill for the man. Only by being obvious could he hope to avoid capture. He had to fit in and making a fool of himself was the only way to do it.

Jonrod turned to him and asked in a low voice, ''Is that your illusion? The big, furry spider? It's good.''

''Be glad to share it.''

''Really? You support me so strongly for Lord?''

''I oppose them.'' Lan lifted his chin and indicated the tiny knot of soldiers.

''I see,'' said Jonrod, stroking the stubble on his chin. ''We have much in common. Are you fleeing them?''

''Yes.'' Lan saw no reason to lie. Jonrod had committed himself as opposing Claybore's troops. Still, a shifty expression crossed the candidate's face only to be masked by his painted-on public smile. He spun and turned back to his crowd.

''A vote for Jonrod is a vote for illusion! Everyone deserves illusions. Why should only the rich be allowed into the park? I'll give every common voter—every one who votes for me—even better thrills than are to be found inside Knokno's precious park.''

That sparked audience delight.

He continued making exuberant promises until his battling illusions faded away. But by this time, the soldiers had also gone. Lan Martak breathed a sigh of relief.

Jonrod finally turned to him and said, "Let's go to my campaign headquarters and discuss this further. I do like your skillful manipulatings of this." He reached out and stroked along Krek's leg. The spider flinched away, mandibles clacking in ominous warning. "Very nicely done," congratulated Jonrod. "Sound, texture, sight. Hard to do all at once. I ought to know. I've made a lifetime's work out of illusioneering."

Lan walked along briskly, watching for more soldiers. They arrived safely at Jonrod's headquarters. His workers—if there even were any, and Lan failed to detect any indication there were—had gone for the night, leaving the rooms bare and silent.

"Sit, enjoy some food." The paltry rations Jonrod set out convinced Lan that this candidate had little backing in his attempts to unseat the current Lord of the Twistings.

Still, Jonrod provided some small start. He opposed Claybore's grey-clad soldiers.

"Why do you want the job as Lord?" he asked Jonrod.

"Why? The man is evil, demented, totally insane! Even worse, he's still popular. That makes him a danger to all of Dicca."

"Where does he stand on the civil war being fought?"

"War, what war?" Jonrod appeared genuinely perplexed. But then, Lan decided Jonrod had never had a genuine reaction in his life. All for him was fraud.

"I saw howlers battling in the air outside Dicca. I talked a little to a downed pilot. Somewhere armed opposition to the greys continues. Is the Lord aiding the soldiers openly?"

"Yes."

Lan sighed. The answer had come too quickly for him to believe it. Jonrod agreed simply to win over Lan. He had dealt with illusion so long, he no longer separated it from reality.

"Why do they call you the Flash?" Lan asked, shifting directions in the conversation.

"My illusions. I am a master at flame and brilliant bursts. I'm saving that for election day. The sky will light with my face. It will be the masterstroke that wins me the election."

"What exactly do you win? Lord of the Twistings indicates something called the Twistings to be Lord over."

The man scowled, then said, "You are truly from far off. The Twistings is the current Lord's most potent weapon."

Lan waited for Jonrod to explain further. When nothing more was forthcoming, he asked, "Where are the city's sorcerers?"

"Where? Gone. All gone," said Jonrod. "And glad I am of that, too! They were competition. They refused to join in the elections; they actually insisted on selling their illusions."

"They only did illusions?"

"More. They created slimy, slithery things. Real things." For Jonrod, reality was anathema. "Screeching things that burned in the air and whistling tornados that sucked the air from a man's lungs. Watery beasts and horrid little things that dug around in the earth. They were odious people. Never very friendly or outgoing. Glad to see them leave Dicca."

"They left about the time the soldiers came?"

"Yes, I suppose they did. At any rate, that's when the Lord began cozying up to them. They obey him, though."

"As if he has something they want?" Lan began putting the pieces together. Claybore came to this world for a reason. With the Kinetic Sphere able to shift his skull and torso to any world he chose, something here had to draw him. If the Lord of the Twistings held some part of the sorcerer's body, that would be impetus enough to forge a military presence on this planet.

"Perhaps," answered Jonrod, obviously not willing to commit himself.

"We'll do what we can to get you elected. Are there others opposing the Lord?"

" 'We'?" demanded Jonrod. "You said 'we.' There are others?"

"The pair of us is more than ample for most emergencies," stated Krek.

"Your illusion sounds good, too," complimented Jonrod. "You have excellent control. No wonder you think in terms of 'we.' You must live night and day with this image to have it so much under control. It is most remarkable."

"It escapes my control at times," admitted Lan, a smile darting across his lips. He motioned for Krek to remain silent. The arachnid hadn't liked being referred to as "it."

"Oh, the time!" Jonrod exclaimed. "I am late for an appointment with a very important and beautiful lady. She offers money for the campaign. Do you . . . two . . . wish to remain here while I solicit? It won't take me long."

"I could use the rest," said Lan. "Go on. We'll wait for you."

"Be back soon," promised Jonrod the Flash as he left.

"What a duplicitous little node of a human," observed Krek without rancor.

"Allying ourselves with him—for a while—gives us a base," explained Lan. "And I need some time to read through Abasi-Abi's grimoire. There are some items in it I intend studying that seem appropriate for this city."

He began reading in the book of magical spells, silently chanting, trying to get a feel for what they did and how they operated. He had been lucky to shift the death beam away back in the forest. One small slip and he'd have ended up smoky ruin. There had to be better spells to forestall that particular weapon.

Less than a half-hour after Jonrod left on his money-gathering mission, Krek interrupted the studies. The spider nudged Lan's shoulder with a curved talon.

"What is it?" he asked, annoyed at being disturbed. But he heard the scraping sounds. He jumped to his feet, instinctively whipping out his sword.

The door burst open. The captain of the grey-clad soldiers he'd seen earlier stood in the doorway, a death tube in her hand. The set of her body, the expression on her face, told Lan she'd kill him in a flash of fiery death if he moved a muscle. He dropped his useless sword.

"Good," she said. To a man behind her, she called, "Pay off Jonrod. We have them."

Lan felt rage mounting inside. He hoped that the coin they paid Jonrod the Flash was as illusory as that man's integrity.

CHAPTER EIGHT

Inyx become increasingly haggard and gaunt. Reinhardt—
Luister len-Larrotti—tried to make her eat, but she refused.
She felt like an addict clinging to the image of her dead
husband. She needed it for life, yet letting that image into
her life destroyed her. Inyx tried to muster enough strength
to again attempt escape from Luister len-Larrotti's Fine
Rooms. To no avail. His magics were too strong. Whatever the physical price he paid for such potent magic, he
had every opportunity to recoup his strength.

He ate ponderous amounts of food. His sexual appetites,
not to mention those of the patrons, kept her exhausted.
She got little thrill from making love to her dead husband a
dozen times a day, yet Reinhardt's image still held her in
thrall. Inyx knew this was the product of magics; len-
Larrotti turned real love into equally real bonds on her.

She'd die soon. But not until the man had made a
handsome profit off her.

Inyx had given up crying and merely sat listlessly staring out into Lossal Boulevard at the anxious, lustful faces
peering in at her. The man kept up a constant flood of
illusion to entice prospective customers. Inyx no longer

cared. Her spirit had been beaten down too many times—
and over all loomed the illusion of Reinhardt.

She heard voices arguing outside her door. She didn't
care. Odissan had returned, expecting to be denied his
money. Luister len-Larrotti had paid. She had earned her
captor much. But with Odissan came a new voice, one
equally as commanding as the loan arranger's. That air of
haughtiness rang out and brought Inyx from her stupor.

"I want her, Luister. Now."

"Odissan told you about her. He wants my Fine Rooms
for himself. I paid that spittin' bastard. You two are in this
together."

A thud told Inyx that the visitor had struck len-Larrotti.
She doubted the fat man could easily regain his feet. The
door to her room opened and, looking past, the scene
confirmed her guess. Luister len-Larrotti lay asprawl, his
head cocked to one side. Blood trickled from the corner of
his mouth while red bubbles welled up along his split lip.
With one punch her saviour had removed len-Larrotti.

Her eyes left the supine form of her captor and worked
upward. The grey cuffs told her what she feared most. By
the time she came to the gold stars and red crosses on the
man's sleeves, she knew.

Claybore's commandant had found her.

"I am Alberto Silvain," he introduced himself. He
bowed gracefully from the waist, his dark eyes never
leaving her. "It is my privilege to be commander of the
guard for this world."

"You're one of Claybore's flunkies."

"You might say that. I would say that my position is
somewhat elevated from mere flunky, however. I control
this world for Claybore. He gives me free rein."

"The Lord of the Twistings rules in Dicca."

"The Lord rules much of this world. It is to him, in
fact, that I am taking you. He tires of the long hours spent
in campaigning. He desires some little diversion. Word
had reached him of Luister len-Larrotti's Fine Rooms.

What a nice idea this is, creating an entire ambience for sexual congress. It had never been tried on this scale before, for whatever reason."

"The locals aren't too inventive."

"Yes, there is that," he said, nodding in agreement. Inyx took in a deep breath, then released it slowly. Alberto Silvain had just admitted he was not from this world. Like so many of Claybore's commanders, he had been trained elsewhere, then offered a world. He had walked the Cenotaph Road, also.

"They live in illusion," the dark-haired woman went on. "It blurs their minds and keeps them slaves to the Lord."

Silvain laughed harshly. "That is only part of it."

"You're taking me to Claybore?"

"Claybore is . . . elsewhere. I am in complete charge. I feel your presence in the Lord's court might cement the already great friendship between two great rulers."

"Claybore and the Lord of the Twistings," Inyx said bitterly.

Silvain smiled urbanely and only nodded. He indicated that Inyx was to precede him from the room. She watched carefully for an opening, but Silvain was not only sophisticated in manner and attitude, he was a cautious soldier. He gave her no chance to escape.

Inyx kicked Luister len-Larrotti as hard as she could when she came to his fallen, bloated form. The man grunted, then rolled to protect himself. She jumped when an electric crackling sounded and a beam of lambent radiance touched len-Larrotti. He shrieked, then died, a hole burned completely through his torso. Alberto Silvain snapped the cylinder he held back onto a ring in his belt.

"The Lord awaits you" was all he said.

Inyx lifted her chin and stalked out. Silvain had robbed her of her revenge against Luister len-Larrotti. For that, if nothing else, he would die. She vowed it.

*   *   *

"There aren't any walls around the palace," she said in wonder. "Doesn't the Lord of the Twistings fear for his life?"

"Walls are needed only by despots. They can keep you in as much as they keep something else out," observed Silvain. "The Lord has much more powerful allies to guard his palace."

She saw immediately what Silvain meant. While the man's outward facade never changed, she felt him stiffen slightly as the slavering beasts attacked. Fully twenty feet tall, the creatures waved small, ineffectual hands in front of them. The real horror came in their powerfully muscled jaws. Clacking shut with fearful determination, those knife-edged teeth threatened to rend and rip and dismember.

And the hunger in those beasts' eyes was more than she could take. She involuntarily cringed and stepped back. Silvain moved so that he interposed his body between her and the creatures.

The man laughed, but it wasn't an easy laugh.

"Those are only illusion."

"I was almost killed by a tiger image in the park. Illusion can kill."

"On this world, you are correct," he said. "Do not forget it. The Lord controls these images. If he had not desired your presence, they would have torn you apart."

"Would they have eaten, also?"

"They're only illusions," he said, shrugging. "If it pleased the Lord to have them dine, they would. Otherwise, he'd tire of their antics and go play elsewhere."

They entered the front doors of the palace. Inyx had seen more opulence and bad taste in designing a ruler's residence, but never had she seen that opulence shift and change even as she watched. She had the passing sensation that all this was unreal, that if she reached out and grabbed, the jewels would turn to mist and the gold would melt like butter in the noonday sun.

She tried not to be too obvious about watching Alberto

Silvain, but every time she glanced in the commandant's direction, she found him staring back. His bold hazel eyes locked with hers, mocking, teasing, tormenting. If he hadn't been one of Claybore's henchmen, Inyx knew she would have found him attractive. As it was, she didn't even try to estimate the murder and rapine and misery he must have caused to rise to such exalted rank.

A man like Alberto Silvain had killed her Reinhardt.

Inyx turned her attention away and tried to lose her thoughts in studying the palace. While it gave her a moment or two of interest, she found her mind wandering. Mechanical servants, all similar to the park manager Knokno she had found on her first day in Dicca, scurried about, clanking and rattling on their rounds. A few humans loitered, but she saw very few that didn't have a military bearing. While they did not wear the grey she'd come to associate with Claybore, she guessed these palace hangers-on were more devoted to Alberto Silvain than to the Lord of the Twistings.

"Yes," Silvain said softly. "The Lord has few loyal to him anymore."

"What if I tell him?"

"Go on." Silvain laughed harshly. She wondered what sort of man this Lord of the Twistings might be. Silvain had obvious disdain for him, yet a tiny corner of his courage crumbled when the Lord was mentioned. A contradiction. With luck, she might turn this into a wedge between grey and Lord.

"Commandant Silvain, you are expected," said a mechanical ludicrously dressed only in a wine-red crushed velvet jacket and a perfectly knotted black silk neck scarf. He bowed slightly as Silvain ushered Inyx into the audience room.

At first she thought she'd entered the palace nursery. Toys littered the floor, tiny windup mechanical devices that scurried like metallic rats when set in motion, blocks of all kinds, even stuffed toy animals. Inyx blinked and raised her sight to room-sized transparent cubes. Five of them contained particularly devious mazes through which animals ran. She swallowed hard. The nearest one contained a creature disturbingly human in shape, although the size belied anything more than a distant cousin. Its gaunt face pressed against the inner surface begged her for release. She stepped forward and touched the barrier; it didn't yield. Inyx rapped it sharply with her knuckles. Only dull echoes sounded.

"It's unbreakable. Watch." Silvain took out his death tube and pointed it directly at the creature. A lance of fire gushed forth and slithered along the flat surface. "Examine the maze wall," the man ordered.

Inyx touched the spot where the heat had been most intense. Not even a blister marred the surface. Inside, the homunculus shook with silent tears.

"The Lord enjoys constructing these mazes," said Silvain. "He is most adept at it. The laws of the outer world are suspended inside. That was once . . ."

"The former Lord of the Twistings," came a high-pitched, almost feminine voice. The giggles that followed turned into a twittering that made Inyx very uneasy.

She faced the newcomer. The voice sounded twelve, the body looked four times that. Dressed in a jester's outfit, the Lord pranced about, posturing and doing small tumbling routines for her amusement. She wasn't amused. Inyx thought this was some trick that Silvain played on her. This fool couldn't be the ruler of most of this planet. She started to speak when she saw the expression on Alberto Silvain's face.

That tiny corner he reserved for fear unravelled into a large spot. He feared the Lord of the Twistings. Mixed in with it came a large portion of disgust, also. That emotion Inyx shared with Claybore's commandant. To lock up any creature in the glass maze seemed unnecessarily cruel.

"You like my tiny mazes? You should see my big one."

"The Twistings?" she guessed.

"Oh," cried the Lord, clapping his hands, "I was so

right in having Alberto bring you here. You are *bright*. Most of the people I see are stupid.''

''Why don't you let out the . . .'' Inyx turned and indicated the homunculus in the maze. It had already moved on, feeling its way around unseen walls, seeking an exit.

''Let out my predecessor? Oh, no, good lady, that would be silly. It took a great deal of magic to reduce him to that size. Once he was released, I couldn't watch him blunder around in my maze. Besides, he treated me shabbily when I first arrived in Dicca.''

She stared at the man. He had a small spot going bald on the top of his head. The light brown hair had been frosted through with grey and lay back straight from his high domed forehead. Chocolate-colored eyes darted and danced with mischief, the eyes of a small child. In stature, the Lord of the Twistings proved average in every way: height, weight, strength. There seemed little extraordinary about him. Except for one thing.

Alberto Silvain feared him.

That puzzled Inyx more and more. Silvain did not frighten easily. She'd seen his type on any number of worlds. They followed their beliefs to the death, never compromising. In a way, their deaths provided more cenotaphs than any other. They died nobly and usually in some fashion where their handsome bodies weren't recovered.

And Silvain feared the Lord of the Twistings. Why?

''I have many, many more intricate mazes about. Come and look at them.''

''That's not a suggestion, is it?'' she asked. Silvain shook his head. She felt his strong hand in the small of her back, urging her forward. This brief pressure gave her the opening she'd sought since being rescued from Luister len-Larrotti's Fine Rooms. Inyx moved, turned, caught Silvain's wrist, and jerked hard. The man cartwheeled in midair, to smash hard into the marble floor. A whooshing noise told her the wind had been knocked from his lungs by the sudden fall. Inyx scooped up the death tube from his belt and stepped back. She pointed it directly at the Lord of the Twistings.

"Oh, what is this?" he asked in a small voice. "She threatens me. Oh, this is rich. It is, it is!"

"No threats. I wanted to warn you about Silvain—and Claybore."

"I know all about them," he said, his eyes sparkling.

"Then you know they're out to depose you."

"No, no," he said, laughing so hard he had to hold his sides. Bells rattled and the metallic stars on the sleeves of his yellow and red outfit reflected back all the colors of the rainbow as he shook. "You have it all wrong. I use *them*. They do my every bidding. Without me—and what I possess—they are nothing. Nothing!" He started laughing again.

Inyx frowned. This dolt thought he manipulated Claybore. From what she'd seen of the sorcerer, that wasn't very likely. Still, Silvain hadn't shown only contempt for this odd ruler of Dicca.

"Do put away that silly toy. I have ever so many more interesting ones."

"Sorry, Lord, but this is where I leave you. Play with Alberto, if you have to have another victim for your mazes."

"No, I want you, good lady. You're different from the others. There's a vitality that won't let you stop till you've worked through my most intricate mazes."

"I'm going," she said firmly. Inyx knew how to deal with children, even ones old enough to have grandchildren.

"No."

Inyx reacted quickly but still moved seconds too late. A thick plate rose between her and the Lord of the Twistings. She spun and tried to run. She smashed headlong into another barrier. In all directions she met resistance. Clinging to the cylinder she'd taken from Silvain, she sought the grey-clad soldier. At least his death might be fact. That'd slow down Claybore's conquest a little.

Alberto Silvain struggled to sit up—outside the glass barrier.

She fired. Inyx felt heat billowing up from the point of contact between lambent energy and transparent surface. She stopped firing and examined the wall. It hadn't been marked. Outside, the Lord of the Twistings helped Silvain to his feet. All the while, the Lord cackled like a rooster and bounced up and down like a child waiting for the spring fairs.

"Isn't this wonderful?" he chuckled, moving close enough to press his face against the wall. His nose flattened and his cheek turned white, transforming him into a grotesquery. She hammered futilely at the wall. The Lord pulled back, a big smile crossing his face. "You have one hour to escape my maze. One whole hour, because this one is my finest, my favorite, my best—my worst!"

Inyx whirled and saw the beast slithering up toward her. Tentacles waved in the air, tentacles laden with needle-sharp spines. It wobbled and squished forward. She fired the tube. The creature vanished as if it had never been there. And it hadn't. It was only illusion.

Inyx heaved a sigh of relief. She faced images.

"They aren't all illusion," came the Lord's soft voice. "No, not at all!"

She began working along the outer wall, turning sharp corners until she was positive she had circled back to her starting point. She hadn't. The dark-haired woman felt a small panic begin. The inside of the maze appeared larger than the outer dimensions. But that wasn't possible. Or was it?

Inyx stepped forward. Her foot touched a faintly discolored portion of the marble floor. Shock raced along her nerves. Excruciating pain snapped her head back and caused her teeth to rattle. She fell heavily. The death tube clattered across the floor.

"You can pick it up," the Lord said, cavorting about just inches away on the other side of the barrier. "Go on."

She reached out and again felt the pain lash every nerve in her body. This time she hadn't touched the discoloration on the floor, only invaded the air above it.

"Better hurry, good lady. Look what wants you for dessert."

She screamed. The monster had no distinct form. It shimmered in and out at the limits of visibility, but what Inyx saw horrified her. Teeth: long, sharp, carnivorous. Eyes: small, red, mean. Talons: meant for ripping apart exposed bellies. Worst of all for her was the knobby organ sprouting between the wavering creature's legs. Tumescent, it thrust forward like a fleshy sword.

"It's hungry, good lady," came the taunting commentary. "And I just fed it three of my meatiest guards. Now, whatever else can it want? For dessert?"

Inyx felt claws raking her body. She fought back, but her hands discovered nothing to grip, to use for leverage. The woman panicked when the beast bent her forward, its claws cutting through her clothing and leaving her bare and bloody.

"It used to be human," said the Lord. "Well, it used to be close to human. I've altered it since I found it in a lower dungeon. We get along quite well, the two of us. I do hope you two will find some enjoyment together."

A needle-sharp talon rested between Inyx's breasts. The creature guided her so that she faced away from it, using the talon as a goad. She screamed when it probed upward between her legs. Fear took control of her as the woman felt the creature violate her.

Then shock set in. A cold, emotionless calm descended on her. Almost as if she were in a daze, she still knew what to do, how to act. Inyx reached between her legs and found a leathery sac tightened with lust. Grabbing it, she jerked forward. The creature bellowed in rage, tried to withdraw. As it straightened, she hooked her right instep behind its foot. Pulling hard on both foot and scrotum, she twisted the creature around. It fell heavily directly onto the spot in the maze which had induced such pain in her earlier.

It cried out, its shrill scream going beyond the upper limits of human hearing. Then it sizzled, wiggling as if it had fallen onto a hot griddle. Its death throes were relatively peaceful.

Inyx clutched her arms around her body and sobbed. The fugue state had passed totally; she had returned to normal, and the reality didn't suit her.

"Why, this is astounding. You are the first to ever kill one of my creatures inside a maze. Remarkable! I knew Alberto had found me a choice prospect. But do hurry, good lady. You have only a small fraction of the hour left to find a way out."

Inyx shot the Lord a look of pure hatred. He delighted in it. She picked up the scraps of her clothing and managed to cover enough of herself so that she felt less vulnerable. Then the woman began to think seriously about the maze. It extended further than it should in the small space. While it had to be magically inspired, the clue lay in the apparent size of the homunculus—the former Lord of the Twistings—she'd seen in the other maze. While the current Lord looked full-size to her, a complex magical spell might have reduced her in size. If so, the maze seemed relatively larger to her.

She considered the dimensions. It might be as much as four times as large as she thought, if she'd been diminished in size. Inyx set out with this in mind, following the outer wall. The turns came where she expected. She heaved a sigh of relief at this. Any information had to be useful. The woman rounded a corner, stopped, and irrationally began to weep.

Spinning, she retraced her steps. The tears continued rolling down her cheeks, but the emotion producing them vanished.

"Ah, the Vale of Tears," said the Lord. "That's one of my better creations. Have you found Laughing Valley yet? Several of my most recent guests have died laughing there."

Inyx didn't answer. She took a firm control of herself

and plunged through the area causing the welling of tears. On the other side, she found her left arm hung limp at her side. No amount of massage convinced it to respond. Inyx felt as if all the nerves had been severed. She kept the general plan of the maze in mind; to blunder around aimlessly meant only death or further misery. She continued walking.

"No more time, good lady. No more. Sorry." She glanced outside. The Lord of the Twistings grew in stature.

Her mind struggled with that. He didn't grow, he was standing up. He'd been sitting down as he followed her through the maze. She was on a bottom level. She had to be.

Searching overhead produced the answer. A rectangle, edges barely visible, stretched above her. Inyx jumped, caught the edges, and pulled herself up. For a moment, she wondered if she'd bettered her position at all. Huge floating eyes stared at her. Inyx gasped, then realized they were the Lord's eyes, peering through the side of the maze. Somehow he had blanked out his face, leaving behind only the brown eyes surrounded with oyster-white sclera.

"No!" the Lord of the Twistings cried. And Inyx knew that finding one extra level to the maze had been the secret for escape.

She raced around, hands pressing into the outer barrier. She quickly found an empty spot.

"Got it!" she exulted. Inyx plunged through the opening. Pain ripped through her body, searing every nerve and causing her to twist and jerk in excruciating agony.

The Lord of the Twistings' laughter soon drowned out her own pitiful cries for surcease.

CHAPTER NINE

"Don't use that," said Lan Martak, holding his hands in front of him, as if to prevent the woman from firing her death tube at him. "This is all a mistake."

"No mistake," the grey officer said. She hadn't risen to the rank of captain by being stupid. "You and the spider are the ones Silvain ordered arrested." She paused, cocked her head to one side as if appraising Lan and finding him wanting, and finally asked, "How did you escape so easily from Zol and his patrol?"

"Zol?" Lan asked. His fingers tried to tie themselves into knots. He felt power beginning to flow. Gently teasing it, he wanted to delay the woman as long as possible until he got a good grip on his spells. The deflection spell required too much concentration; it welled up from deep in his unconscious mind. He had to employ another spell if he wanted to get away unharmed.

Power surged. He reached, almost controlling it, almost making it his own.

"The leader of the troops at the cenotaph. Zol's a good man. You hardly appear the sort to get by him."

"He frightened much too easily," said Krek, his voice louder than normal. "All I did was—"

"Stop!" the woman barked. She swung her tube toward Krek. This was the opening Lan needed. He took a pace toward her.

"Don't harm him," he said, pulling her attention back from Krek. "He's a bit simple-minded."

"Simple!" The spider's mandibles clashed horribly. But this time her attention remained on Lan. She had figured out what the man had tried to do—she wasn't going to allow him to take even one step more toward her without firing.

"Enough talk. We go to the palace. The commandant wants to speak with you."

"Can't do it," said Lan, advancing. The woman's finger tensed on the trigger. He kept moving. She fired.

"Friend Lan Martak!" shrieked the spider. "You are hit!"

The beam went straight and true—and missed his body by several inches. Lan felt no pang of chivalry as he danced forward and squarely planted his feet. His fist drove short and powerful for her chin. Her head snapped back. She fell to the ground, unconscious.

"But I don't understand," said Krek. "Her death beam struck in your rather scrawny midsection."

"I've been reading up on illusions. I'm not too good, but I did find one that was easy enough to conjure. I made her think my body was shifted a foot to the right. The beam hit an illusion."

"You might have informed me you were going to do such a thing. It is unseemly for me to carry on as I just did." The spider primly pulled himself upright, back and abdomen brushing the ceiling.

"No time for that. She's brought her soldiers with her."

"I fail to see what problem that presents."

Krek bellowed, then charged—directly through a wall.

A cloud of plaster filled the air as the spider rushed out. Screams of terror quickly drowned out Krek's battle call. Only one grey-clad held his line. Even so, his shaking hand barely held his cylinder. As he brought up the weapon to fire on Krek, Lan triggered the death tube he'd taken from the fallen woman. The beam lanced forth and speared the man. He died before his body struck the ground. If the other soldiers had been willing to fight, the sight of their captain unconscious, Jonrod the Flash's building in ruin, and one of their own number cut in half on the street dissuaded them. They broke and ran.

"Let's get out of here," Lan said, tugging at the spider's hind leg. "Some officer's going to wonder why they're running around without supervision; then all the demons of the Lower Places won't be able to help us."

"Quite," said Krek, composing himself. "Let us explore in *that* direction." He indicated the opposite direction from that taken by the soldiers.

"It's remarkably easy avoiding them," said Lan, ducking into a store as a small patrol of grey soldiers went by. "The election has them tied up too much to pay any attention to individuals." He glanced at Krek, who stood silently by, lost in his own thoughts. With the campaign heating up for Lord of the Twistings, more and more illusions stalked the streets. In comparison to any of them, Krek now seemed to be minor, insignificant, not worth a second glance.

"Where are we?" asked Krek. "We wander aimlessly and for too many days. This pavement tires my feet. When you have eight feet, it does not pay to have even half hurting."

"Sorry, old spider," said Lan, without too much sympathy. "Ever since we left Jonrod's headquarters a couple days ago, I've been trying to section off the city for a systematic search. We've gone through the majority of the places I think Inyx most likely to be."

"This is Lossal Boulevard," said the spider. "I recognize it from our first day in Dicca. The part we traverse is much seamier than that we previously explored."

"You want anything or did you just come in to pee and get out of the sun?" asked a gruff shopkeeper. Lan looked around the shop and decided he didn't have much appetite for pigs' ears or ox eyes, both considered gourmet items by the Dicca gentry.

"Need information," he said. "A few days back someone told me about an illusion along Lossal."

"Nothing but, these days," the man grumbled.

"These were Fine Rooms. A window display."

"You mean Luister len-Larrotti. Humph." The shopkeeper spat and accurately hit a spittoon, making a brass ringing noise. "Son of a sow keeps his damned unsightly place a few blocks farther south. Past Mittervault Avenue."

"Nobody seems to like this Luister len-Larrotti, but everyone knows him," observed Lan. "He must be something of a local villain—or celebrity."

"Spit, that's what he is, spit." The man demonstrated. "But this is a perky one he's got in his window. Or so I hear."

"I'll check it out and report back firsthand," promised Lan. He and Krek left. Outside, Lan said, "He's been by those Fine Rooms. I can tell. But he's like most of the people around and won't admit it. This must be some sight."

"Your libidinal instincts are much too esoteric for me to ever understand, friend Lan Martak. We spiders keep our basic lust on a high, pure plane."

"And then your mate eats you."

"Every culture has its drawbacks," Krek said primly.

"Come on. Let's find Luister len-Larrotti and his magical Fine Rooms."

As they walked, Lan noticed more and more mechanicals in the streets. They performed most of the menial chores and many of the more demanding ones. He'd never discovered where they were constructed nor how they were powered. Trying to detect any magical power source had failed completely. Lan wished he had the time to properly study the leather-bound grimoire he carried and learn more about such things. He was positive he lacked the skill to detect the spell powering them rather than some other form of motivating energy being used.

"They clank," came Krek's terse comment as a pair of mechanicals swept the street clean of debris following one of the more boisterous election speeches involving much confetti, cheering, and illusions performing incredibly erotic activities.

"They also don't need food, can work around the clock without tiring, and seem much more intelligent than the majority of the citizens likely to vote for Lord," said Lan.

"That is not difficult. These humans are so image-befuddled they no longer separate fact and fantasy. Living daily with their fondest dreams robs them of their spirit."

"I agree," said Lan. "I wonder if the mechanicals can vote in the election."

"If so, they ought to vote for one of their own kind. None of the humans I have seen is worthy of leading a slop-bucket brigade, much less running a city."

"Lord of the Twistings encompasses more than Dicca. The post rules most of the planet, from the way they talk. And not a one has mentioned the war going on."

"Friend Lan Martak, look!" the spider cried. Such a burst of emotion from Krek stopped Lan in his tracks. For a moment he wondered what the arachnid had seen.

Then he saw, too.

"Inyx!" he shouted.

Furry legs smothered him, twisted about him, held him back. He fought. Krek tightened his grip until Lan realized he'd never be able to fight free. Even his berserk rage didn't give him enough strength to match Krek's.

"Let me go. I won't do anything stupid."

"You tried," accused the spider. "They outnumber us by a considerable margin."

Lan struggled to his feet, getting free of the coppery fur on his friend's legs. He half-hid behind Krek and peered around. His hand went involuntarily to the death tube swinging at his belt. Reaction still brought out his sword when the combat promised to be close, but he had slowly retrained himself to think of the tube when the enemy appeared more than a few yards distant.

"In the window," said the spider.

Lan Martak went white. For a moment, the blood rushed from his head and he felt light-headed. Then anger caused blood to rush back. He flushed and only a great control of will prevented him from making a suicidal attack.

"Luister len-Larrotti," he said, the name coming out as a curse. "He used *Inyx!*"

"So it seems," said the spider. "No wonder the attraction was so potent for those along Lossal. Inyx is a comely female—for a human. However, please remember, friend Lan Martak, you were quite willing to gawk at someone else."

"They won't get away with this," muttered Lan, under his breath.

The grey-clads snapped to attention when a tall man escorted Inyx out. Lan eyed the man, burning his every feature into memory. His stomach sank as he began itemizing: the man was good-looking. He carried himself with an air that spoke of decisiveness, and Lan knew that the soldier was nobody's fool. Those cold eyes missed little as they scanned the crowd arrayed around len-Larrotti's Fine Rooms.

"He did not see us," said Krek. "They travel further south on Lossal."

"We're following them," said Lan. "I've lost Inyx in the whiteness between worlds. I lost her for almost two weeks on this damned planet. I'm not going to lose her now!''

They trailed along, only a half-block separating grey-clad soldiers from Krek and Lan. Lan fingered his swinging death cylinder, considering, calculating, evaluating his chances. The time wasn't yet right to rescue Inyx.

Dammit!

CHAPTER TEN

Inyx screamed in abject agony. Every nerve in her body exploded in a pyrotechnic display of pain. She writhed about, kicking, moaning, sobbing. When she thought there wouldn't be any way to survive another instant of the excruciating pain, it mounted and a fresh wave of torture wracked her. She didn't know how long she was lost in that wasteland of pain. A second. A day. Her guess was eternity.

When the woman began to recover, she found that her limbs hadn't been broken into a million pieces, that her intestines hadn't been pulled out and strung around the room, that she was completely intact. Inyx sat and checked herself carefully. Not even a scratch.

"Ho, good lady," came the now-familiar mocking, shrill voice of the Lord of the Twistings. "Wasn't that just about the most delightful experience?"

"What happened?" she asked. Her body had been freed of pain; her brain remained clouded with the memory.

"You found the way out of my favorite maze. Oh, it was exciting. Seldom have I experienced such enthusiasm for a subject. You are the first to discover the secret of that maze.''

"I am, eh?" She fought to control the mad rush of her pulse, the hammer of blood in her temples.

"It's not finished. Yes, that's my little secret. I haven't had time to construct more than one level of the maze. Getting up and out of that plane allows you to leave.''

"The pain," she mumbled.

"A small indication of the barrier spell, nothing more.''

Nothing more? Inyx rolled to hands and knees and paused there for a moment, regaining her composure. It proved difficult in this animallike position. Her tattered clothing fell off her, leaving her more naked than clothed.

"You are also the first to figure out so quickly how I compact so much into the tiny space available. Why, the former Lord of the Twistings still hasn't figured it out, and he's a sorcerer!''

The Lord giggled and started turning handsprings. On the last one, his hand slipped on the marble floor, sending him crashing into an ornately carved oak table. He picked himself up, laughing boisterously. To all outward appearances, the Lord of the Twistings was a buffoon, a complete and total fool. Inyx knew better. However he acted, a shrewd and capable mind backed his actions.

She had no doubt that the Lord was completely insane. That didn't prevent him from being brilliant. If anything, it made him even more dangerous.

"Come, look at my other mazes. See this one. I'm just now building it.''

Inyx cautiously followed. The Lord ignored her hesitation and raced forward, cavorting and pointing out the more gruesome particulars of his already-built mazes.

"This is a special favorite," he boasted. "Only one percent of all those put in ever live. And they aren't worth much after a few days. It gets so tiring trying to find those who can survive my intricately constructed mazes.''

Inyx felt her stomach churn at the sight of tiny people struggling along inside the maze. They had teamed up to fend off the maze creatures the Lord of the Twistings sent after them.

"This was the first maze in which I exclusively used the nerve-deadening trap. I've since learned to direct it toward particular parts of the body. Like so."

The lead figure in the maze, hardly more than six inches tall, suddenly vented forth a shriek of miniature anguish and clutched at its thigh. Inyx couldn't tell if the victim was male or female. It didn't matter. What counted was the Lord's outrageous sadism.

"The people of Dicca elected you to do this to them?" Inyx asked. "Why don't they take you out, strip the flesh from your living body, and let the crows peck away at you?"

"That's interesting, but uninspired," he said in an off-hand manner. "How about flaying off the skin, dipping in salt and acid, *then* letting the crows loose? Or perhaps cut worms. Yes, that's much more interesting. Cut worms."

"If any of the others is elected, would they change all this?" she asked, motioning to the playroom.

"Oh, certainly they would, certainly they would. Take Jonrod the Flash, for instance. He'd never play with miniature mazes. He'd do away with all these in a flash—and reserve a place in the Twistings for his enemies."

Inyx felt sick to her stomach.

"Then there's that silly slut Clarita Zannermast. She'd ruin everything I've worked so hard to build here." The Lord started to pout at the thought of anyone else being elected. "The ignorant slut. Why, she's told me—confidentially, of course—that she'd make all this public. Imagine sharing these fine excursions into the human condition with the *masses*. Really! She'd share this, make it all open to the gawking, unappreciative electorate."

"A fine group runs for Lord," said Inyx in a low, cold

voice that might have been nerve-deadened by one of the maze traps.

"The finest. Absolutely the finest Dicca has to offer. That's why I must be especially tactful this year to retain my position. Why, any one of them might unthrone me."

"That will not happen, Lord," came Alberto Silvain's smooth voice. Inyx glanced at him. His dark face still shone with perspiration, and a pinched quality about his lips told of the strain he was under. Otherwise, he was his urbane self.

"No, no, it won't, will it, my good sir? Not with your Claybore aiding me. Not with all those fine grey-clad soldiers rushing about, making certain my opponents don't get too many votes. That just wouldn't do, now would it? And who knows, Claybore might even get what he wants. Wouldn't that be nice?"

"Claybore has only your well-being in mind," said Silvain.

"He's lying," blurted Inyx. "They want what you have."

"Of course they do," said the Lord, laughing so hard he approached the brink of total hysteria. "And they won't get it away from me. Not now, not ever."

Inyx studied Silvain. Determination slowly replaced fear. The Lord of the Twistings had better watch his step around this man. Nobody had such perfect control that one like Alberto Silvain couldn't bring the entire house tumbling down.

"Come, oh yes, come, my good friends. It is about time for the noonday election speech. This one is special, ever so special. You'll both just simply *love* it to death."

Silvain gripped Inyx just above the elbow with a strength not easily broken. He took no chances with her this time. She went along as docile as a lamb. She needed to regain her strength.

Then she'd strike out again.

"This studio is unique to the Lord," said Silvain in a

low voice. "It is his greatest weapon in the fight to get reelected."

Inyx stared in wonder at the mechanicals bustling about the large room. The apparatus they dutifully tended meant nothing to her. One mechanical, the one in charge of the others, pointed. A large hanging on the far wall shimmered and became transparent—or so Inyx thought at first.

"It's a window!" she exclaimed. "On the city. I can see people moving. But . . ."

"It's not merely a window. The 'other side' of that device is miles away, near the center of Dicca. The Lord watches the crowd, waits for the proper moment."

Inyx stared in fascination. Silvain spoke the truth. This wasn't a window in any sense she knew. The people were too large to be distant, yet she had the feeling this picture came from far away. The mechanicals quietly discussed it among themselves, then the scene shifted with dizzying speed. A man harangued a crowd, whipping them into a frenzy with his rhetoric and his illusions.

A hush fell.

"They've seen the screen begin to glow," said Silvain. "Above the platform. They know that when it turns white, that means the Lord of the Twistings speaks."

Inyx saw the Lord strut in. He had changed from his fool's costume to one more befitting royalty. Vivid purple velvet had been lined with delicate furs of white and gold. A blazing silver emblem woven into the fabric over his chest proclaimed his rank, as if it weren't obvious from his haughty bearing.

He clapped his hands and sent mechanicals scurrying like robotic mice. They turned and bowed when all was in order.

The screen Inyx watched carried a replication of the Lord fifty times larger than life. She guessed the impact on the crowd. Such magics were more potent than any mere illusion.

"People of Dicca, people of the world. The election is

soon upon us." He paused for dramatic effect. Inyx found herself breathing faster, caught up in the rhythm of the way he spoke. This man was no fool. He controlled the crowd as easily as he did the miniaturized victims trapped in his diabolical death mazes.

"Many running for this exalted office promise much. They will deliver little. They speak of you in abstract terms. Remember what I have given you. Remember it well!"

Cascades of coin fell from the sky—faery gold. Inyx reached for a piece and it dissolved at her fingertips. She looked at the screen; the crowd enjoyed this teasing approach. They had forgotten totally about the other man on the platform under the screen.

"Illusions. They are not enough. Illusions and reality. These I offer freely. And what is reality? Reality is peace of mind. Reality is a safe feeling, knowing that we are safe in our homes, on our streets, in our most private places.

"Crime has risen." He paused to let the words sink in. "I am not unaware of this sad development in my beloved Dicca. As part of my campaign, I not only offer you coins," and again they fell from the skies, "I also offer the most startling reality. I offer an end to the criminal element. None dares the Lord of the Twistings' wrath . . . if the penalty is banishment."

"Banishment!" came the cry from the assembled throng. "Give them to the Twistings!"

"Yes," thundered the Lord's amplified voice. His fifty-times-lifesize image leaned forward, a stern look crossing his patrician face. "The Twistings!"

The crowd went berserk. They crowed and cheered, they slapped one another on the backs, they rioted. Inyx hardly believed that one word—*Twistings*—inspired such joy.

"Why are they cheering him?" she asked Silvain. The man's face had clouded over with anger. He held back only through duty.

"He's toying with me," said Silvain in an ugly tone. "I shall not tolerate this! I shall never—"

His words were drowned out as the Lord of the Twistings continued his televised harangue.

"I have such a criminal with me. Her master has chosen to die rather than be banished."

"*Banishment!*" shrieked the crowd.

The Lord smirked, then gestured. Mechanicals pushed Alberto Silvain aside and gripped Inyx by the arms. They propelled her to a point five feet behind and to one side of the Lord.

"She lewdly displayed herself in a Fine Room. That is acceptable. But she had the temerity to also do it in public view. She caused a public scandal. The current Lord of the Twistings shows no mercy to those who flaunt the law. What should be her punishment?"

"*Banishment!*" the crowd responded, on cue.

"To the Twistings," he said, with an imperious wave of his delicate white hand.

"What's going on?" demanded Inyx. "What kind of a trial is this? I was forced to do those things. Luister len-Larrotti made me!"

"To the Twistings, to the Twistings!" chanted the crowd.

Inyx failed to read the expression on the Lord's face. It was a curious mixture of loss—of a plaything?—and revenge and triumph. She remembered what Silvain had said. The Lord toyed with the soldiers' leader. She provided a convenient pawn in this power struggle, nothing more. She'd given the Lord a few minutes of sick pleasure while trapped in his diabolical maze, but this transcended personal enjoyment. He now struck out at Claybore and Silvain, used her as a tool in his reelection, and doomed her.

The Twistings.

Whatever that meant, it boded ill for her.

"Shut off the sound," came a low command. The

mechanicals obeyed. From where he stood, the Lord told her, "Enjoy your vacation. You were most diverting."

"Where?" she asked.

"Stop this, Lord," demanded Silvain.

"Stop it, Alberto? Stop it? Hardly. Unless you want to join her, you'll be quiet. But then you *do* want to join her, don't you? Shall it be now? Is that your plan, Alberto?"

"The Lord knows that justice is his." Silvain bowed and backed away. Inyx hated Claybore's commandant as much as she could any human being, but she had the feeling of loss. In some fashion she didn't comprehend, she'd just lost a powerful ally in her battle to stay alive.

The mechanicals dragged her away.

Down halls, past closed doors, descending stairs, she quickly lost track of direction. She was being taken to the lowest levels of the palace, of that Inyx was sure. They moved so fast that Inyx knew she'd have been lost even with a detailed map of the route. The mechanicals said nothing, but even in their metallic visages she detected a sadness—and a fright.

"If you see him, tell him we still think of him," whispered one to her left.

"Quiet," barked another. "He listens in."

"Knoton," said the first mechanical. "Tell him we still remember him."

"What are you doing?" the dark-haired woman demanded. They stopped, opened a door, and pushed her through. She stood, staring. A long corridor ended in another door, a huge vault door. In the center of the shining barrier smiled a likeness of the Lord of the Twistings, retouched to make him appear much more handsome than he was.

"Forward," commanded one of the mechanicals. A well-placed hand in the middle of her back sent Inyx stumbling. The heavy vault door swung ponderously, hinges silent and well oiled. A sharp sulfur tang came from the other side, the odors of hell.

"I won't—" she began. The mechanical shoved her

again. Off balance, Inyx staggered through the portal. For a moment, she wondered if this were only some insane method of imprisoning her. The room in which she stood was barren, devoid of all furniture, decoration, or even texture. The vault door closed with an ominous click.

Inyx turned to examine the room further. As she moved, the world reeled about her. She dropped to her knees, feeling as if she had shifted between worlds, using a cenotaph. Colors flowed in wild kaleidoscopes, sounds starting below her range of hearing, then crescendoed upward till her head almost split. She felt, she tasted, she heard and experienced . . . damnation.

The woman spun through space and time, tumbling, lurching, jerking, twisting, especially twisting, forever twisting inside and out.

Inyx knew she had truly found the Twistings.

CHAPTER ELEVEN

"Bigger than life," muttered Lan Martak. "This is similar to the projection device used by the Suzerain back in Melitarsus."

"Larger," said Krek. "And the Lord of the Twistings is not as personable."

"Personable," snorted Lan. "That woman tried to imprison us. Even if it was a prison of gold and fineries."

"Note how he controls the crowd with his voice. Seldom have I seen a more consummate politician," said Krek. "This is a touch of magic. Perhaps not in the sense you mean when you chant spells, but it is magic, nonetheless."

Lan had to agree. The Lord built the crowd's emotions to a fever pitch, then stopped just short of inciting them to riot. Then he began again, teasing and tormenting them, moving them along in the direction he desired. The poor campaigner who had been on the platform under the giant screen when the Lord of the Twistings appeared had become a nonentity. No one noticed him now, even with his colorful illusions cavorting about, performing increasingly obscene acts. Lan turned back to the Lord's immense face when the other office-seeker stopped his erotic images and left the platform in disgust.

"Crime is vicious," the Lord said, as if he stated a newly found truth of the universe. "Only punishment befitting the crime will stop the rampaging rise of offenses against the public."

The crowd screamed. The picture altered from the Lord's face to a long hallway with a huge vault door at the end. The people around Lan and Krek fell strangely silent at the sight. The silence spread until Lan heard only his own heart beating. Over fifty thousand people stood without making a single sound.

"The Twistings," explained the Lord. "This is my weapon against crime. Cast the criminal in!"

The crowd sucked in and held its collective breath in anticipation. Lan's eyes widened in recognition when he saw whom the mechanicals shoved forward.

"Inyx!"

"Be silent, friend Lan Martak. If you let on you know her, they will rip you to bloody pieces."

He didn't need Krek to tell him that. He raged at the sight of the mechanicals shoving Inyx past the vault door, then closing it. The last view he had of her was standing in a bare room, a perplexed expression on her face. The scene changed to the exterior of the vault door, cunningly painted with a smiling portrait of the Lord on it.

In everything, the Lord advertised himself.

"Such will be the fate of all criminals. The Twistings!" came the disembodied voice.

"The Twistings! The Twistings! The Twistings!" The throng screamed until Lan's ears revolted and refused to listen.

He grabbed one of Krek's back legs and pulled the spider from the plaza. They sought out a back alley and slumped against the cool walls of the buildings. Only when a ringing note in his ears came did Lan speak. His voice sounded hollow, distant. He was still partially deaf from the intense noise of the crowd's cheers.

"What do we do now?" asked Krek.

"Go after her."

"These Twistings that so fascinate the crowd do not appear to be easily visited," the spider pointed out. "Such a venture on our part might be dangerous or even suicidal."

Lan knew his friend was right. What did he owe Inyx? He turned that question over and over in his mind. He had gotten her into this fix, at least indirectly. Without his interference with Claybore she would have never become lost in the whiteness between worlds. Still, he had rescued her from that fate. Whatever drove her into Dicca and the Twistings wasn't morally his burden.

Yet he felt it was.

Did he love Inyx? Lan Martak had no easy answer for that one. They had fought side by side. Did this shared blood constitute love? He doubted it. Rather he felt an admiration for her, a loyalty to her. She was definitely a friend.

Maybe more. Maybe.

Lan looked up at the silent bulk of the spider. He had fought and killed for Krek. Krek had done likewise for him. Yet as close as they were, something was lacking in their friendship. He guessed it was Inyx. When the three were together, they functioned as a whole, a unit, something transcending individuals.

Did he love Inyx? Yes. But mixed in with that love were other emotions no less powerful.

"We can't leave her," he said. The decision made, he felt a weight lift from his shoulders. They might march into the Twistings, into death, but the attempt to rescue Inyx had to be made.

"So we retrieve her," said Krek.

They started for the palace of the Lord of the Twistings.

"No wall," said Krek. "I have not been able to spin a

worthwhile web since we came to this miserable world. I had hoped to be able to dangle freely, swinging to and fro, from the tallest spire of a castle. But this, this is pathetic!''

Lan worried, but for different reasons. Any ruler accumulated enemies, those who had been turned down for jobs, those defeated, those ruined, even the insane. From what he had seen of the Lord of the Twistings, the man probably required constant bodyguards. The position was coveted by many; assassination had to play a major role in this world's politics. It did everywhere else.

"There aren't any guards to be seen, either," Lan pointed out. "It can't be this easy. We don't just walk in."

"He might prefer an open-door policy when dealing with his adoring populace."

"He might prefer being buggered by a dwarf," snapped Lan. "There are guards around. There must be."

"What of magical wards?"

"Nothing. I don't even feel the generation of any illusions."

"I see none," said the spider. "There is one sure way of finding if our senses lie."

"Krek, no!" he called, but the spider began walking across the grassy lawn toward the palace. His rolling gait didn't vary as he approached the nearest building.

Lan swallowed hard and followed. Halfway across the lawn, he felt his body from the waist down go numb, as if his spine had been snapped. Falling forward, he began dragging himself with his hands. He wanted to call out to Krek but refrained. A momentary burst of magic had told him ward spells did exist; he was too unsophisticated to detect them until it was too late.

To his surprise, the paralysis vanished within a few feet. Lan crouched, running his hands over his legs, enjoying the tingle as his fingernails cut into flesh. He turned and studied the terrain he'd just walked. By deep concentration he "saw" a spot on the lawn. Unlike a perpetual guard spell, this was somehow triggered mechanically. His weight had set off a debilitating spell. How the Lord mixed physical with psychic Lan had no way of knowing.

Turning his tuned sense forward, he "saw" several other patches dimly glowing. Avoiding those brought him to Krek's side.

"There were traps in the grass," he said.

"Oh? I found none."

"There are benefits to being eight-legged—and long-legged, at that. Any of the traps you might have triggered sent a column of energy directly upward. Your body stays well away from where your feet are placed."

"Keeping all my feet beneath my body as you humans do is obviously impractical."

Lan began a retort, then froze. He heard a name mentioned that sent a thrill of discovery throughout his body.

Claybore!

He motioned to Krek. They picked their way closer to the building, then edged along the wall. Lan "saw" several more of the traps and indicated Krek should pass them by also. With contemptuous ease, Krek stepped over the magically glowing spots.

"But Claybore," came the protest from inside a palace room, "he did it on purpose. I had no chance to oppose his action, not in front of half the city."

"Silvain, you disappoint me," came Claybore's familiar voice. Lan peered in. The soldier he'd seen escorting Inyx from Luister len-Larrotti's Fine Rooms hunched over a box. Wavering inside the box was a blue wraith—Claybore's skull.

"Do you wish me to lead a force into the Twistings?"

"No! Not yet. That part of me residing with this upstart's maze is important, but not vital."

"How goes the search for your tongue?" asked Silvain, obviously desiring a change of topic.

"It is difficult. The village chieftains require much persuasion, but I am hopeful that the information I require will soon be given. With my tongue once again in my head . . ."

"You will be invincible," finished Silvain.

The cold chuckle Lan remembered all too well filled the room, echoing, reverberating, building to a horrific pitch. The wavering blue mirage inside the box shook from side to side in negation.

"Not invincible. But certainly more powerful. To again be able to enunciate certain spells. That will speed the conquest. I need the freedom of a tongue to chant those spells most desired."

"May your quest be successful," Silvain said earnestly.

"And yours, Alberto, may it also be successful. I want that part of me returned. Also remember that the woman must die, as must the man and the bug."

Lan placed a restraining hand on Krek's nearest leg.

"It will be done."

"I am sure it will. I place complete trust in you, Alberto." The dancing ghost-image inside the box crumbled into nothingness. Alberto Silvain leaned back and wiped sweat from his forehead.

Ducking down, Lan said softly, "Claybore is already at work in another world. Whatever it is of his body left on this planet can't be too important, not if he is leaving it to a subordinate."

"Silvain appears competent enough."

"Claybore doesn't take chances," Lan said. "I got the feeling that whatever they want is . . . Krek, run for it!"

Lan Martak spotted a patrol of grey-clad soldiers marching in precise step. Their officer had already located them before Lan shoved Krek in the opposite direction and shouted his order.

The soldiers had been trained well. Their death tubes sprang to hand. Lightning bolts slashed through the air in front of the fleeing pair, bringing them to a complete halt. Lan's mind raced as he tried to figure out what had gone wrong. Getting into the palace undetected had been easy. How had they been detected?

Krek silently lifted a leg and pointed toward the sky.

Fluttercraft circled above, far enough away so that the sound of their rapidly spinning blades didn't reach the ground but not so far away they couldn't spy on every square inch of the palace grounds.

Lan's mind tumbled and churned in agitation, preventing him from attaining the concentration required for casting any of the spells he knew. Even if he had been able to divert the death beams from himself, there wasn't any way he could protect Krek, too.

The soldiers maintained position, cylinders pointing directly at their targets. Striding through their rank came their captain, smiling broadly. Lan knew he had reason to be happy: he'd just fulfilled Claybore's command to capture the "man and the bug."

"The commandant has been expecting you," said the officer. He bowed and indicated Lan and Krek should precede him.

Lan walked off. To face death.

CHAPTER TWELVE

The sensation of falling through infinity vanished, only to be replaced by one of spinning. Inyx staggered like a drunk, reaching out for support and finding nothing. Colors flared and odd odors assailed her nostrils. Whining deafened her, and her skin dripped ichorous fluids that made Inyx nauseated simply from the feel.

The assault on her brain ended as quickly as it had begun. Inyx stood in a hallway. Behind her was nothing. Ahead, the same. Which way had she come? No indication of passage told the tale. She dropped to hands and knees and began checking the floor in both directions.

Nothing.

An examination of the walls failed to disclose any hidden doorways. The floor appeared substantial, and the ceiling, while peeling yellowed paint, looked solid.

For all intents and purposes, she had entered a bare room, turned, and ended up in the middle of a very, very long hallway with no obvious entry point.

"Well, I'm alive. I've been in worse places." She tried not to think of the almost-dead quality between worlds. Inyx looked left, then right. "Which shall it be? To the left.'' It mattered little since no differentiation was possible.

Inyx walked. And walked and walked. For hours she walked. No doors. No cross-corridors. No one.

''So this is the horrific Twistings,'' she muttered. ''The Lord bores his victims to death with the sameness of it all.'' Her words echoed slightly, then died. Coming in on top of the echo, however, her sensitive ears detected a . . . chomping.

Inyx looked behind her. A light blue bulbous creature, more teeth than body, waddled along, filling up the entire corridor. Its massive jaws swung open, revealing an impossibly large mouth. The jaws closed with a bone-jarring crunch. It advanced. The jaws opened.

Inyx ran.

The beast whined in triumph and speeded up. She stumbled, braced herself against the wall, and kept running. Her fastest was barely enough to stay in front of the opening and closing mouth. Once, when she slowed down the tiniest fraction, hot breath gusted along her neck and the chomping sound came too close for safety. Tiny bits of skin stayed on the teeth; Inyx picked up the pace.

She came to a branching in the corridor. To the left, she noticed the floor had been littered with small yellow globules. Trying to hurdle them and stay ahead of the blue gobbling creature didn't seem too conducive to long life. If she remained in the same corridor, the path was clear. Inyx kept on the straight and narrow.

Only when she'd gone another twenty paces down the hall did she venture a look behind. The hungry beast stood at the junction, turning to face the perpendicular corridor, then back toward Inyx. It made a decision and walked off on tiny legs toward the yellow globes. It vanished from sight.

The woman gasped and leaned against the wall, arms around her own body. Safe. For the moment.

''I was wrong about you, Lord,'' she said when she

regained her wind. "You're not the kind to be content boring me to death. You're trying to run me to death." And, she silently added, scare me until my heart explodes from the fright.

The paths open to her didn't seem too appealing. To continue meant more of the same. Going back only covered terrain she'd already seen, even if it had been at a dead run. Curiosity enticed her to the juncture. Peering around the corner, she saw the blue monster gulping up the yellow globules. The sight of the creature feasting set her own stomach to rumbling. She couldn't remember how long it had been since she'd eaten. From Alberto Silvain she had gotten nothing. Her last real meal had been a drugged one given her by Luister len-Larrotti.

If the blue beast ate and survived on the globular fruits, so could she. The only problem was stealing one away from the creature. It had picked the hallway clean and made a right-angle turn some distance away to vanish from sight.

Cautiously, Inyx followed.

Her careful advance saved her life. She heard the gulping, snuffling sounds in time to turn and run. The round blue appetite had doubled back and now pursued her. Inyx ran, skidded around the bend in the tunnel, and stopped. Coming toward her were wraithlike creatures. The lead one glowed an incandescent red. Behind came one of a more subdued sea-green. Eyes burned like insanity and tiny hands groped in front. To her left came the blue glob. She had only one way to flee.

Inyx took it.

Unholy screeching noises echoed past her as she ran. She turned and saw the blue spheroid attacked by the leading wraith. To her surprise, the contest was one-sided. In spite of the teeth and voracity, the blue ball had no chance.

Inyx slowly learned the hierarchy in the Twistings. And she had to class herself as being at the bottom.

* * *

The wraith hovered at the juncture of two corridors, facing away from her. On silent feet, Inyx advanced. Her hands reached out. With a movement more like a striking jungle cat, she caught the wraith around the spot where its throat ought to be. Inxy felt substance; the creature only looked ghostlike. She leaped, her legs circling the beast's body. Her weight and ferocity forced it down. The dark-haired woman found what passed for a throat, and cut off wind.

It took over three minutes to strangle the wraith. It took even less for her to discover it wasn't edible.

The corridor stretched as far as the eye could see, strewn with the yellow fruits. Weak and shaking from lack of food, Inyx still took the precaution of checking the cross-corridors for any sight of either wraith or blue eating monster. Nothing.

Hungrily, she picked up the nearest globe and bit through tough skin. The warm pulp inside dribbled down her chin, over her tongue, and into her throat. She spat out heavy pink seeds without taking her mouth away from the succulence of the fruit. Inyx ignored all conventions of politeness and decency. When the fruit had been messily consumed, she went on to another and another. Eating so much fruit might eventually give her the runs—it also saved her life.

The sugars triggered energy sites in her body. She felt her head clearing. No longer dizzy and faint, she rose, wiped away the pulp from her mouth and tunic, then picked up one of the cannonball-sized fruits. It proved semiportable.

"No!" she cried. Inyx sighted another of the blue monsters. It entered the hallway and began devouring all the fruit leading to her. She had learned that they never passed up a meal. This gave her time to escape, clutching a single fruit for some future meal.

She found another juncture and ducked into it to avoid several wraiths drifting toward her. The same sensations she'd experienced entering the Twistings caught her up again. She spun and whirled and finally dropped to her knees—in a different part of the Twistings.

Never had Inyx felt more helpless.

Voices. Humans' voices. She debated about seeking them out or fleeing. Then the hard thought came to her: she couldn't run for the rest of her life. Alone, unable to sleep, she'd soon fall prey to the beasts scouring the Twistings for food.

She squared her shoulders and walked forward. For a moment, she thought she'd been transported to still another world. In a large room—the first she'd seen in the Twistings—sat or lounged at least fifty men and woman.

All were filthy and wore tattered clothes, and not a few were quite insane. Some sat staring into infinity and gently humming to themselves. Others carried on detailed conversations with no one.

". . . vegetables deserve their freedom," one man was saying. He spun, his voice lifted and he answered himself, "Scallions are vegetables, too. What about them?"

Inyx sidled past this human remnant while he continued the debate with himself. She knew who the loser in that discussion would be. Others rocked to and fro like zoo creatures in a cage, while still others fought with a ferocity that belied their humanity.

"A new one, eh?" came a sober voice from her right. Inyx glanced in that direction. A blonde woman, with arms around drawn-up scratched and bruised knees, peered at her. The blue eyes were a bit wild, but the inflection in her words came out saner than anyone else Inyx saw in the room.

"I was just put into the Twistings today." She stopped, frowned. "I think it was today. I seem to have lost track of time. I got hungry, found this, then I . . . I spent a lot of time running away.''

"The fruits are about all that's good for eating. With one exception,'' said the woman. She inclined her head to indicate the far side of the dimly lit room. A fire blazed in the distant corner and two men roasted a haunch of meat. The odor wafting in her direction made Inyx's mouth water.

"I suppose they want more than to be friends to share,'' she said.

"You can be their friend—or more—if you like. Not too many want to share their meal.''

Suspicion flared. Inyx inhaled more deeply of the odors. For a moment, she didn't recognize the meat the two men cooked. Then she blanched. Once, when women and children had been trapped in a burning building, the stench of tar and wood had been intermixed with burning human flesh.

This odor was similar. The only difference was in intensity. These men roasted, not burned.

"Don't want to share their meal anymore?'' asked the blonde.

"I think I'm going to lose what little I have eaten.''

"Share the fruit?''

The blue eyes fastened hungrily on the fruit Inyx held cradled in her arms like a small babe. Inyx wanted to say no, to keep her hard-won food for herself.

"Fifty-fifty,'' she said. "If you've got a knife to cut through this leather.''

"No one's got a knife, 'cept the mechs. And they cannibalize their own parts for them. Teeth'll be as good as anything else. Go on, you do the divvying.'' The blonde watched as Inyx carefully bit through the tough skin. Juices spurted. With great care, she divided the fruit and passed over the larger section to the blonde.

"Thanks,'' the woman said even as she thrust the savory pulp into her mouth.

All too soon, they'd finished their meal. The blonde sat licking fingers and blouse for the last of the juice.

"How long have you been in the Twistings?" asked Inyx.

"Can't say. No one knows. We just wander aimlessly."

"Is there a way out? Does the Lord have the entrance blocked with anything other than the vault door?" She tried to remember the door itself. Most vault doors protecting vast caches of money tended to be difficult to open from the outside but relatively simple to burgle from the inside. Inyx hoped this might be the case with the Lord's door into the Twistings.

"Some have found the room again."

"How'd they get out?"

"Out? They came back. Over there. See that one, the one with the red hair? She sits and cowers if anyone approaches her. She told me that she found the door open. All she had to do was walk out—and she couldn't do it."

"Why not? I'd be through that door in a flash."

"No, you wouldn't. I heard that same story million times or more." The blonde played with one of the pink seeds. She stroked it as if doing so gave her some magical power. It was only a nervous gesture.

"I would!" said Inyx with heat. "I want *out* of here. And when I escape the Twistings, I'm going to kill the son of a bitch who put me in here."

"You won't care, not after a while. No one does. Only the newcomers try to escape."

"Giving up hope isn't the answer. If she found the way out, so can we."

"Why bother?" The blonde leaned back, relaxing only slightly. She kept her arms around her knees. The blue eyes looked at Inyx again, hungry once more but this time with a different form of hunger. "We can do other things, you an' me. You're not wonky yet. Neither am I. We can . . . do . . . things together, we can."

"I want to talk with the redhead," Inyx said, uncomfortable now with her nearness to the blonde. "What's her name?"

"Don't know. Can't even remember my own. What's the difference?"

Inyx rose and walked away from the blonde. The woman called out, "Thanks for the food."

Inyx waved in response and hurried to the redhead. "You almost escaped," she said without preamble. "How'd you do it?"

The woman gazed up at Inyx, then smiled. Inyx shivered at the insanity she saw in that look.

"Easy. Just followed my nose. But I couldn't . . . couldn't leave. Couldn't."

"Why not? What kept you in the Twistings?"

"Don't know. Couldn't walk out the door. Tried." She began laughing, high-pitched and hysterical. This brought unwanted attention from the two cannibals at the far side of the room. Inyx backed off, wanting to run. She managed to find herself a quiet spot along one wall where no one seemed willing to stay. Hunkering down, she tried to think her dilemma through. Somehow, the more she worked on the immediate problems of getting out of this crazy maze, the more difficult it became for her.

She cried herself to sleep, visions of blue gulping beasts that turned into humans haunting her dreams.

The clatter of steel on steel awoke her. She'd heard enough fighting in her day to know the sounds of battle. One raged very close by. Inyx craned her neck, searching for the source of the noise. Off to one side down a dimly lit corridor seemed the most likely spot. The residents of the room had begun slipping quietly away from that point, not wanting to fight.

Inyx flexed her muscles, winced at the way she'd stiffened during her sleep, then moved forward. Dying in battle was preferable to rotting away physically and mentally.

Even being devoured by a wraith or globuloid had to be a more fitting death for one used to freedom.

"Back," came a warning. "Get back. Knoton's coming. He's going to clean out the entire nest."

"Nest?" she asked. The man stumbling along had been bloodied by a dozen cuts, none deep. He had risked much bringing the warning—and he didn't seem as demented as the others she'd met.

"The room. This place." He staggered forward another few steps, then stared into her deep azure eyes. "You've just arrived. Too bad. Knoton's coming. He's going to kill all us humans this time. And the hybrids, too."

"What are you talking about?" she demanded.

"Knoton's a mechanical. He hates all flesh and blood for exiling him to the Twistings."

"But we're here, too!" she protested. "That's not fair."

"He's not quite sane, either. But in this place, who is?" He grabbed Inyx by the shoulders and spun her around. "Now get moving. Knoton'll be here in another few seconds."

"We should fight."

"With bare hands?"

Inyx peered into the gloom of the corridor the man had just vacated. Shining spots began growing in size. Mechanicals made their way forward, brandishing knives and swords. If any of them had been the shining perfection she'd seen in Dicca, Inyx would never have risked battle. But these mechanicals were rusty, slow-moving, clanking. Their banishment to the Twistings hadn't been good for them, either. She waited for the first pair to enter the room—the nest, the man had called it. Then she acted.

She dived forward, dropped to support her weight on one arm, then scissored her legs around the lead mechanical's. A gyroscope whined, the mechanical struggled for balance, then fell heavily. Inyx quickly recovered the fallen sword. She noted it had been made from another mechanical's arm.

Even the metal men were cannibals in the Twistings.

"Watch out!"

She heeded the man's warning by ducking. Just a fraction of an inch over her head slashed the other mech's long knife. Inyx recovered balance, measured distance, lunged. Her blunted sword point found a spot between spinning cogwheel and shoulder joint. The mechanical whirred in rage, turned, and succeeded in forcing the sword even more deeply into its shoulder workings.

Inyx tried to continue her attack, but the mech held her at bay with its knife. Her human companion aided her now. A swift blow to the mechanical's back threw it off balance. It sagged, allowing Inyx to wrench free her now bent and dulled sword.

Together the two humans decapitated the mech. It twisted fitfully, struggling to recover its cranium. Inyx let it pick up its head, then scuttle off for repair. The sight of the headless body brought back unpleasant memories.

Claybore. His skull floated without benefit of body.

"Good fighting," complimented the man. "You're the best warrior I've found since the Lord threw me into the Twistings a couple months ago. I'm Fredek Fynn."

"Fredek, the pleasure's all mine. I'm Inyx."

A metal-on-metal screech deafened Inyx. She threw her hands over her ears to dampen the noise. She succeeded only in part.

"What was that?" she said, louder than she'd intended.

"Knoton's battle cry. A challenge. Let's get into the maze, where we have a chance."

Inyx's reluctance to leave this room and enter the maze almost overwhelmed her. Then the dark-haired woman saw a battle in progress. Down the corridor two shadowy forms locked in mortal combat. One was mechanical—Knoton. The other appeared human until a random flash of light reflected off silvered arms.

"The arms," she muttered, unsure of what she saw.

"A hybrid. Knoton hates them worse than he hates flesh-and-bloods like us," said Fredek.

"We should help," Inyx said weakly. A strong hand rested on her upper arm. Fredek Fynn pulled her away.

"There's nothing we can do. Look at it this way. Whoever that is just gave us a few more minutes of life. Knoton's on a war-binge. Nothing short of disassembly is going to stop him now."

Inyx curtly nodded. She and Fredek trotted for the far side of the nest. The sword resting firmly in her hand gave the woman a feeling of safety now, even if it was a false one. No sooner had they entered the corridors than they ran afoul of a blue gobbling beast. It waddled forward, snapping, and gnashing its teeth.

"Don't try to kill it," warned Fredek. "Even with a sword, it's hard to injure. Make it mad and it's well-nigh invincible. They don't ever seem to feel much pain."

"I killed one of the wraiths with my bare hands," said Inyx. "With a sword, I can kill this thing."

"You killed a *capper*? Great Twistings, I've found me a real she-demon!"

Inyx pushed the man out of the way to clear the way for a lunge. She executed the attack perfectly. The blunt tip of the weapon, however, inflicted minimal damage. At the last possible instant, she changed the next lunge into a devastating slash. Ichor flew in all directions as the blue monster chattered in rage and pain. It launched a frontal assault that Inyx simply couldn't stop.

She and Fredek retreated back into the nest.

From the other side of the room, Knoton shrieked his metallic cry of rage and vengeance. He lumbered forward, swinging a steel rod easily seven feet long.

Inyx and Fredek Fynn were trapped between the injured blue globuloid and an equally blood-crazed mechanical.

"Now!" shouted Inyx. She shoved Fredek one way and dived the other herself. Blue maze monster and mech faced one another. Knoton's towering hatred drove him forward, metal bar whistling as he swung it in long, angry arcs. The creature had been blinded by its own blood.

It attacked.

Inyx watched in silence as the awesome battle raged. Knoton refused to give ground. His rod battered the tough blue skin repeatedly until Inyx was positive nothing solid could remain inside. But still the blue maze creature fought on, its teeth clattering off the metal rod every time it managed to get a chance to snap. Such stark ferocity couldn't be maintained long. By the time Inyx circled and met Fredek, the metallic had triumphed over flesh and blood and voracious appetite.

Knoton stood, left arm bitten off, one eye blinking wildly, his right leg bent at an unnatural angle.

"I shall destroy you. I shall destroy all human life in the Twistings for what that madman has done to me!" the mechanical raged.

"Knoton," spoke up Inyx. "Let's parlay. Let's declare a truce and talk this out. We're all here because of the Lord."

"He's flesh; so are you. You shall die, soft one!"

Knoton wheeled around and limped away, leaving behind miscellaneous nuts and bolts. It would have been ludicrous except that Inyx looked past the hardware to the dead maze creature.

In the distance she heard the wraiths—the cappers, Fredek had called them—coming. Hunger in the Twistings was a way of life and death.

Silently she and Fredek left the nest. There'd be time to return later, after the cappers had fed.

CHAPTER THIRTEEN

"So good to see you," Alberto Silvain said, rising from his desk in the cramped office. He extended a hand in friendship toward Lan. Lan refused it. Silvain smiled even more broadly and turned to Krek. "Will you accept my hand?"

"Only as part of dinner," said the spider. "As a rule I am not overly fond of flesh. In your case, I make an exception."

Silvain laughed delightedly.

"Such wit, even in the face of death. I admire that. Yes, I understand why Claybore worries so about the likes of you." He joked and bandied words with them, but all the while Lan Martak felt the cold, calculating stare he'd come to expect from one of Claybore's ablest, most cunning subordinates. Silvain was no one's fool. He hadn't been placed in charge of all the grey-clad soldiers on this world because of his white smile.

"Why has Claybore rushed off to another world, leaving you behind? Is the cause here so hopeless?" asked Lan.

"Attack, never rely on defense. Yes, I like you more and more, Martak."

"He left you to fight a rear-guard action."

"Nothing of the sort, as you probably already know. This world is pleasantly under control. It no longer requires Claybore's personal attention. I rule in his place."

"This must come as a shock to the Lord of the Twistings," said Krek. "From the intensity of his campaign speeches, he believes he governs this world."

"The Lord is an annoyance we accept, nothing more," said Silvain, his mood darkening to match his swarthy complexion. "He is a fool to be tolerated—for the moment."

"Does he know how you feel?"

"Martak, how the Lord of the Twistings feels is of no real concern. As long as he has his pretty mazes to play with, he is content. The day-to-day rule in Dicca and elsewhere is in the control of my officers. Any decision that is made, we make. Is that clear?"

"What does he have that Claybore wants?" asked Lan.

"Borgo, were they spying when I contacted Claybore?"

"I do not know, Commandant. The fluttercraft patrol spotted them, then alerted me. I captured them near your window."

Silvain turned back to Lan.

"So, you overheard as I spoke with him. Then it's no secret that Claybore seeks out still more of his body elsewhere." Alberto Silvain studied Lan for a moment, then added, "The body on this miserable mud ball is of little value."

"That's why he entrusts you with recovering it?" asked Lan. He felt the soldiers behind him stiffen. One tiny flick on the trigger of their death tubes and he'd be smoking ruin. Still, his position was hopeless unless someone made a mistake. Better to try now than wait for Silvain to be surrounded by hundreds of his grey-clad soldiers.

"Claybore warned me that you have a sharp tongue. And a sharp wit. You shall not anger me so easily. In fact, you shall not anger me at all. Borgo, take them out and kill them both. I want evidence brought back to me that my orders have been successfully . . . executed.''

"At once, Commandant!"

Lan tensed to make an escape. A dive through the window seemed almost suicidal. Any other course definitely had death marked on it. But before he got his legs gathered under him for the attempt, a peremptory shout echoed in the tiny room.

"Halt! The Lord of the Twistings demands their miserable presence immediately.''

A mechanical dressed in a pale green tunic and nothing else pushed its way past Silvain's guards. Lan saw Borgo turn to face the newcomer. Lan kicked out, his boot connecting with the man's elbow just as he raised the death tube in the mechanical's direction. The virulent beam tenaciously gnawed its way through plaster, support columns, and part of the bookcase as it fired harmlessly.

"Silvain, put a leash on your man," came the mechanical's harsh command.

"Borgo, never mind," said Silvain with great reluctance. "You will get your chance later.''

For the span of a dozen heartbeats, no one moved. The mechanical eventually faced down Borgo, who slung his tube back onto the carrying ring and shoved his way out of the room.

Only then did Lan breathe any easier.

"Both of them. The human and the spider. Bring them at once to the Lord's audience chamber. He expects them to be in good operating condition." The mechanical pivoted and walked away on well-oiled bearings.

"You take orders from a pile of iron now?" Lan asked lightly. He still probed for the point where he gained advantage over Silvain. He didn't find it.

"Take them to the Lord's audience chamber," Silvain said, disgust dripping from his every word. "I'll join you there shortly. I must report.''

He turned back to the small box on the table. Lan "felt" the identical sensation he associated with a cenotaph opening. The inside of the box glowed a faint blue. As he and Krek were taken out, he caught a fleeting glimpse of a fleshless skull he remembered all too well. Alberto Silvain had contacted Claybore once more.

"So big. This one's so big. I can hardly touch his body. Look." The Lord of the Twistings jumped as high as he could. His fingers stopped just short of Krek's abdomen.

Krek shifted uneasily, weight rocking from side to side. He wasn't used to anyone trying to touch him.

The Lord cavorted about, doing his somersaults and scramblings on the glassy, slick inlaid tile floor. He rolled to a sitting position and smiled ingenuously at his captives.

"You look so upset. Don't be. I'm very nice. I'm very nice to everyone. Ask all my friends."

"What about Inyx?"

"Inyx? I don't know her. No, I haven't heard the name."

"You're lying," said Lan, barely keeping his anger under control. The Lord took him for a fool by playing the fool. He'd seen this man's campaign speech on the giant screen. There hadn't been any trace of a buffoon then. Now he acted like a man missing the grey stuff between his ears. "You sent her into the Twistings."

"I did? Oh, perhaps I did. Was she the one who did so marvellously well in my tiny little mazes? The mazes in my playroom?" The Lord stared at Silvain.

"Yes, Lord, she is the one."

"Such a bright girl. So smart. She worked her way through my little maze in no time at all. That's why I have a new maze. Do come and look at it."

Lan and Krek had no choice. The guards surrounding them made sure of that. Lan looked about in surprise when he entered the Lord's "playroom." Head-tall mazes lined the walls. They reeked of magic, those transparent walled mazes. He reeled under the impact. Whatever spells had been used to form the mazes, they were potent ones.

"You have a little of the magic yourself, don't you?" the Lord asked shrewdly. "Perhaps the girl had it, too. Perhaps that's why she so easily escaped. But not even she could find her way out of this one. It's special," he said in a low, confidential voice.

"Special in what way?" Lan asked.

"I'll show you!" Like a small child with a new birthday toy, the Lord clapped his hands and bounced up and down excitedly. "You. Into the maze."

The soldier stared aghast when the Lord of the Twistings pointed at him. He pulled out his cylinder in a reflex action when several mechanicals moved in to seize him. The human fired twice and two of the mechs vaporized, leaving behind little more than rubble and the sharp tang of metallic gas. The others, however, closed from behind, grabbed the man's arms, and hoisted him off his feet. Kicking and shouting curses, he was tossed onto the top of the transparent box.

Lan felt the magics begin their work. The man sank slowly through the top, seemed to fall into an infinite well. Diminishing in size until he appeared little more than six inches tall, the guard clung frantically to his death tube. When he smashed into the floor inside the maze, Lan began to understand the spells used. He might not counter them, but he knew how the Lord of the Twistings accomplished them.

"Yes," said the Lord, watching Lan rather than the man in the maze. "An interesting experiment, this one. Look, witness, learn!"

Inside the maze the guard fired his death tube in vain. The energies began to wane. Soon the cylinder hung useless in the guard's hand. Then began the real torment. At every turn, the man screamed in silent agony. His flesh began boiling and blistering. His eyes exploded as if someone had stepped on them. He bent and twisted as bones broke. Lan felt his gorge rising as he saw the anguish the man underwent.

"Stop it," he said in a low voice. "Why are you doing this to him? He didn't do a thing to you."

"Don't you like it?" The Lord pouted. "And I worked so hard, I really did work hard, on this. Why, I've got the only plans for releasing someone from this maze. Do you want to know a secret?" The Lord bent closer in a conspiratorial fashion. "He'll live forever. Yes, he'll live forever unless I say the right words."

"Like that?" Lan fought to keep from vomiting. The man inside the maze underwent continual tortures no human should ever face.

"Like that. Forever. Only I can release him—in a very special way."

"Do it. Do it, damn you, do it!" Lan shouted.

"Beg some more. I like it. I really do like it."

Krek roared and surged to his full height. Mighty legs driving, he sent mechanicals and human guards scattering like so many toy soldiers. His serrated mandibles clacked ferociously as he attacked the side of the maze. But even his razor-sharp mandibles failed to scratch the surface of the maze.

"Oh, this is so much fun!" chortled the Lord. "So much fun. I *do* enjoy you both so. In fact, I enjoy you both so much, I'll give you one wish."

"Release the guard," said Lan without hesitation.

"Done." The Lord of the Twistings closed his eyes, murmured a soft chant, then gazed into the maze. Lan recoiled when he saw twin beams of ruby light blaze forth from the man's eyes. Claybore wasn't the only one controlling that spell, it was now obvious. The dual beacons of death slid past the barrier, into the maze, and washed across the man's minuscule form. He stiffened, tossed fleshless hands into the air, then *sifted* down into a pile of black ash.

"He's free."

"I meant for you to release him."

"Oh, you don't understand. There is no escaping this maze. Once inside, there's no way out. Unless you have the plans." The Lord of the Twistings sniggered as if he'd told the most bawdy joke ever. He clutched the small blue book containing the plans to his chest as he rolled over and over on the floor.

"Is death so funny?" grumbled Krek.

"No, but you two are. You could have asked for your own freedom. Now you must stand trial. Yes, that's it. You must stand trial!"

"Lord, this is a farce. Do away with them now," snapped Silvain. "Allow me to handle this."

"You would deprive me of my fun? Never!" The Lord kicked out and sprang to his feet, his hands never touching the floor. In spite of himself, Lan marvelled at the man's agility. Still, what else did the Lord of the Twistings have to do day in and day out but practice his gymnastic tumbling?

"Lord," began Silvain.

"Silence! To the audience chamber. We shall hold the trial immediately."

Krek and Lan Martak stood off to one side, out of the way. The Lord of the Twistings dominated the proceedings, standing dressed in his regal uniform of state. He paced on an elevated stage where every angle was covered by one of the cameras.

"Record it all, yes, record, record, record!" the Lord said to his mechanicals. "If this proves as interesting as I think, it shall be used in the campaign. The electorate will love it. Yes, they'll simply lap it up."

"Silvain," called out Lan. The commandant turned a sour expression toward him. "What's going on?"

"He plays still another of his games," came the sullen answer. Alberto Silvain barely held his temper in check. "It matters little. You will be dead. The only question is when."

"On stage. All the jurors on stage." The Lord clapped

his hands. For a moment, Lan didn't understand. The creatures parading onto the stage weren't human—or at least most of them weren't. The mechanicals were decked out in black ribbons tied securely around their throats. The two humans had on little more. There was a third type that Lan identified—a combination of mechanical and human. One had a human torso with mechanical arms and legs, while another had the reverse. Somehow, seeing a metallic body with human arms unnerved Lan.

"Similar to the mechanical contrivance Claybore used to transport his skull from place to place," observed Krek.

Lan glanced at his friend. The spider sat unconcernedly amid the tangle of his eight legs. His head bobbed slightly from side to side, but other than this he displayed no outward emotion.

"They're going to order us killed," he told Krek. "Doesn't that worry you?"

"You are learning spells from the grimoire," answered the spider. "You will think of some way of disabling the mechanicals. We can deal with Silvain's troops easily enough then."

"I'm pleased with your confidence in me." Lan frowned and began sorting through the spells he knew, trying to decide which was the most effective. But the harder he thought, the more difficult it became. The bizarre congregation on stage stood to one side, making shuffling motions and slapping one another on the back. The metallic clangs as one mech slapped another rang throughout the room and robbed Lan of the needed quiet to formulate his spells. He had no doubt that a master mage worked well in any environment.

He was far from being a journeyman, much less a master.

"Know all here that the Lord of the Twistings calls for justice!"

"Who cares about justice?" muttered Silvain. "I wanted an execution."

"The crime I spoke of earlier continues to run rampant. To show my desire for justice, I have assembled this panel of jurors to find the defendants guilty of their crimes."

"What crimes?" shouted Lan. "We've done nothing but oppose Claybore and his attempts to subjugate your world."

The Lord went on as if he hadn't heard the outbreak. Lan had to admit that it might have been possible. The man worked himself up into a frenzy. When on stage, in front of the cameras recording this for the voters, the Lord became a different person. He had energy, verve, a drive that vanished when he was left to his own devices. Nothing of his sadism showed now. He was the consummate actor playing a lead role.

"Bring the prisoners forward so that all can look upon them and know their villainy."

Mechanicals prodded the pair on stage.

"How say the jury in this matter?" cried the Lord. "Are they guilty as charged?"

One of the hybrids moved forward. His mechanical arm toyed with the black ribbon around his throat as if this might become a noose at any moment.

"Guilty, Lord. Guilty on all charges."

The Lord of the Twistings turned and stared directly into the camera. His face became a stern father-figure mask. He shook his head sadly, as if what he had to do caused him great anguish.

"Guilty. I must sentence them to the maximum penalty allowed."

Lan started to protest, but Krek brushed a furred leg against his arm, silencing him. The man knew that speaking now solved nothing. This hadn't been a trial in any sense. It was a public spectacle, nothing more. To speak up only gave the Lord further exposure.

"Death!" Alberto Silvain lithely jumped onto the stage, drawing forth his death tube. "Allow me to carry out your wise sentence immediately, Lord."

"Silence!" The command froze Silvain in his tracks. "Death is richly deserved for what these two have done. But the Lord of the Twistings is not merciful, will not allow simple death to end it all for them. I protect the people of Dicca, of the entire world! Their punishment must fit the crime."

Lan closed his eyes and swallowed hard. In his mind he heard the crowds cheering and chanting, "The Twistings! The Twistings!"

Only deathly silence filled the audience chamber.

"I sentence them to the . . . Twistings!" The last word hissed as the Lord said it.

"I protest, Lord," bellowed Silvain. "Death. Let me mete out your just punishment of death!"

"Touch that tube of yours and you shall join them, Commandant. You'd like that, wouldn't you? Yes, you would. You could obey your master's orders so much more easily that way."

Lan and Krek exchanged glances. Whatever Claybore wanted on this planet—whatever Silvain had been entrusted to recover—lay inside the Twistings.

CHAPTER FOURTEEN

"Looks the same as it did on the screen, doesn't it?" Lan commented. The vault door leading into the Twistings had been depicted accurately when Inyx had been cast forth.

"We shall be able to rejoin Inyx," said Krek. "If we are allowed to live that long."

Lan walked down the corridor toward the huge vault door. His mind lovingly shaped the spell he needed to turn aside the death blast from Silvain's weapon. The commandant had been fingering the device all the way down from the audience chamber. While he had outwardly agreed to the Lord's exiling them into the Twistings, Lan knew better. Claybore had ordered their deaths; Alberto Silvain would obey.

"Cast the criminals into the Twistings," came the ringing order. Lan turned and saw the Lord standing on a rolling platform pulled by a pair of the juror mechanicals. He'd simply fastened the black ribbons around their necks to the platform. They pulled him the way horses pull carts.

The silver door swung open silently. Beyond lay the simple unadorned room. Sulfurous smells boiled forth. Lan felt the tensions mounting. Silvain had to act soon.

He and Krek were nudged forward by the Lord's mechanical guards. None of Silvain's human troops had been allowed this far.

"Now!" barked Silvain.

Lan's mind reached out, used the spell, strove to deflect the beam from the death tube. Instead of finding the death beam, a heavy metal fist struck him squarely in the stomach. The air gusted from his lungs. He doubled over and fought to keep from blacking out. He looked up to see the mechanicals locked in fierce combat—with each other.

"Rebellion," Lan muttered to Krek.

"Which side do we favor?" asked the spider. Lan had no easy answer for that. To fight on the side of the Lord's loyalist mechs meant they'd be thrust into the Twistings. To fight against them gave Silvain a free hand to murder them on the spot. Lan straightened, kicked a mechanical leg out from under one robotic guard, and backed toward the entrance to the Twistings.

"You said it. Inyx is on the other side. Let's go join her. But first . . ."

He ducked and dodged his way to Silvain's side. The man, for whatever reason, didn't use his death tube. Still, the knife he wielded proved deadly enough to give Lan second thoughts about this impetuous course of action. Then he had no choice. The Lord's side gradually pushed back the mechs opposing them. Lan had to act now.

He grabbed Silvain's wrist and forced the knife up and safely away. At the same time, his other hand groped for the tiny leather-bound grimoire that had been taken from him.

"No, Martak, you won't get it." Silvain gritted his teeth and tensed all his muscles. The man outweighed Lan by a considerable margin—and none of it was fat. At the last possible instant, Lan stopped opposing Silvain's strength and spun about. The action sent Silvain tumbling over and down. Lan grabbed and sprinted for the vault door.

Just as he entered, he heard the Lord laughing.

Then the world twisted crazily and he spun, shrieking, into infinity.

"This is a peculiar place," observed Krek.

"What a wonderful job you're doing if you've just figured that out," Lan said acidly. The disorientation he'd experienced entering the Twistings hadn't been shared by Krek. The spider remained aloof and impervious to it.

"I, at least, did not go hooting and howling off like you. It took considerable effort to maintain your pace, I might add. Never have I seen you travel so fast."

"But the colors, the shapes, the sounds!"

"Nothing," said the spider. "I followed you, remembering every turning, every corridor that you traversed."

"You can get us out again?"

"Certainly." For once Lan didn't care that the arachnid was smug and self-satisfied.

"Let's go exploring, then. I've got enough to get us through just about anything." In the last seconds before entering the Twistings, he'd recovered his grimoire, in addition to stealing Silvain's death tube and knife. With these items he felt confident enough to take on anything the Lord threw his way.

"Something comes," said Krek, his talons pressed against walls and floor. "Something large and slow."

"No problem," said Lan. He pulled out the cylinder, checked to make sure his thumb rested lightly on the trigger, then asked, "Where's it coming from? Left or right junction?"

"Left."

And then the waddling blue monster was on them.

Lan fired point-blank, to no effect. He fired again and again, and still the creature waddled on, filling the hallway so completely that there wasn't any way of dodging. The man didn't have time for even the simplest of magical spells; he'd relied too much on Silvain's death tube. Hacking and slashing with the knife produced little more reaction than had the tube.

Furry legs engulfed him as Krek lunged forward. Blue globe and giant spider slashed and gouged one another. With a quickness that Lan hardly believed, the blue monster spun in the hall and went waddling off in the direction it had come.

"Thanks, old spider. You saved me that time." Lan felt an uneasiness mounting. He turned and saw another creature coming at him from the other way. Still far enough away, it gave him time to formulate his fire spell. He had learned a rudimentary fire spell when very young; it had aided him in the wilds. On his own he'd developed it to something more offensive in the way of weapon. With hints in the grimoire, he thought he might turn it into a formidable force.

Wrist-thick lances of flame blasted forth from his fingertips. Heat boiled back and seared his eyebrows and made his eyes water. Nothing mortal could withstand that wall of fire he cast forth.

Nothing except the blue glob. Its huge jaws opened and shut as if it hadn't even noticed his devastating spell. Lan started to cast the spell again, in spite of the enormous drain it made on his vitality, when Krek stopped him.

"What are you doing?" the spider asked softly.

"The monster. Another one. It . . . it's . . ." Lan looked back. No monster. He gusted a sigh and slid down the wall to sit on the floor. "An illusion. I should have known the Twistings would be filled with them."

"Allow me to ascertain the reality of what we find," said Krek. "My superior arachnid brain is not befuddled like your decidedly inferior human one."

"There's that," Lan said in disgust, "plus you can fight off the real monsters we run across."

"Yes, you are quite right."

"Let's walk. And keep track of where we are. I want to get back out of here as soon as we find Inyx."

"Friend Lan Martak, you worry too much."

They walked. And walked and walked. Lan made no effort to remember the turnings, the corridors, the slightly curving halls they traversed. The initial confusion he'd experienced entering the Twistings made it worthless trying. Still, he learned one thing quickly. Most of the monsters were real. Only a few—usually the wraith creatures—were illusory.

"How'd this maze ever come to be built?" he asked, more to hear his own voice than for a response.

"The Twistings is underground," said Krek. "I can sense the rock above my head, all around. From the 'feel' I get, the corridors were burned out of solid rock, possibly by fire elementals."

"The sorcerers just turned the elementals loose to honeycomb the planet's crust? Why?"

"Who can say what a sorcerer thinks? From association with you and other humans, my best conjecture is that something even more vile lived underground. The elementals burned them out, leaving the tunnels as a by-product."

"And somewhere along the way," concluded Lan, "the Lord turned this into a mind-twisting maze—a prison—for those whom it wouldn't do to execute."

"Possibly this obsession with mazes had a more benign origin."

"What do you mean?"

"Most cultures enjoy puzzles, mazes. I know my own hatchlings enjoy contriving new and more intricate web patterns. Perhaps the original Lord used this as an amusement park, allowing people to wander around until they were tired."

"It's possible, I suppose. They have a park in the middle of Dicca devoted to illusion. Remember how Jonrod mentioned only the rich were allowed in Knokno's park?"

They walked in silence again, not encountering any creatures. The presence, the *presence*, Krek lent to their small party kept most of the maze creatures at bay. Lan came to learn the only ones attacking were the illusions, but he still felt a thrill of fear when they advanced. His magical powers weren't honed finely enough yet to detect image from reality.

After a few hours of hiking, Lan said, "I feel as if I don't want to leave—ever."

"Another magical spell? A compulsion?"

"Maybe so. But another idea comes to mind. The Lord taunted Silvain."

"About something inside the Twistings. Yes, friend Lan Martak, that may be it. Whatever it is of Claybore's that has been lost is within the confines of the Twistings."

"Silvain wouldn't enter himself, not until he was sure he could escape with what Claybore sent him to find. He's afraid we'll find it and destroy it."

"If it is part of Claybore's body, it is indestructible," pointed out Krek.

"For the most part, you're right. But Abasi-Abi had worked for years on a spell designed to get around such protection. I found it in his grimoire. If we can find what Silvain and Claybore are so interested in, we might be able to come out of this ahead of them at last."

The only warning of attack he had was a small scraping sound. Then Len felt the metal dart enter his shoulder, twist, and firmly embed itself on barbed hooks. He slumped forward, the corridor spinning. Whoever threw the missile wasn't an illusion. Lan turned painfully and glanced back, his vision blurring.

A mechanical readied another dart. Lan's finger pressed down on the death tube's trigger. The mech's legs sheared off just under the hip. It crashed to the floor, struggling to bring its dart into play. Lan fired again. The beam lightly brushed the mech's arm. At last only harmless pieces of their antagonist remained.

"Pull it out quick, Krek," he told the spider. Mandibles clamped on the finned dart. He almost fainted when the spider did as he was told. Blood trickled, then gushed from the wound.

"Allow me to bandage it," said Krek.

Lan felt spider silk touching his skin, binding solidly. In less than five minutes Krek had woven a tight bandage over the wound. The pressure directly on the entry point staunched the blood flow until Lan could begin his own healing spells.

The man didn't dare carry those spells too far. It presented him a case of lesser evils. If he completely healed the wound, he'd be too weak from the penalties the magics subtracted from his vitality to be very effective in another fight. On the other hand, the wound itself weakened him. He cleansed the wound magically, then began a healing. When he was finished, he needed Krek's aid in walking. He felt drained, exhausted from the use of the spell.

They went to where the mechanical's face glowered up at them. Lan picked it up and stared into the glassy eyes.

"Why'd you attack? Did you think we were maze creatures?"

"Knoton ordered all humans killed." While it hardly seemed possible, Lan had the feeling the mech looked from him to Krek, wondering if Krek counted as human.

"Knoton's a mechanical?"

Lan got no answer to that. He hadn't expected one.

"Friend Lan Martak, hostility inside the Twistings is more than we expected. I can cope with illusion. We can both defend ourselves against mere physical attacks."

Lan's shoulder twinged in pain.

"You're suggesting we should retrace our steps and get the hell out of here, is that it?"

"Regroup is a better way of phrasing it. We can reenter the Twistings equipped to do battle, knowing what to expect. That will assure us a much better chance of success."

"You're afraid my wound will keep me from fighting."

"There are dozens more mechanicals coming down the corridor," said Krek. "You cannot fight them all."

"We signal one another," said the mech's head. Lan threw it from him in disgust. The head seemed too much like Claybore's fleshless skull for him to tolerate its insolence.

"The room through which we entered is not far distant," said the spider. "Let us retreat, heal, return then."

"Let's go," said Lan. He disliked the idea of stopping, even for a moment, his hunt for Inyx, yet Krek's advice made sense. Even now he heard the metallic feet tramping down the adjoining corridor. Whether or not the mech had lied about signalling them didn't matter. An army advanced on their position, and he and Krek were in no position for holding off warring elements in the Twistings.

CHAPTER FIFTEEN

Sharpened steel blade cut off a lock of her black hair. Inyx dodged the mechanical's next slash, lunged. Her knife failed to penetrate the mech's vitals. She and the robotic creature grappled and fell to the floor.

"Die, human," grated the creature as it struggled to roll on top of her. The woman fought desperately now. She'd been surprised by its sudden appearance, seemingly out of thin air. The mechanical outweighed her by a three-to-one margin. Once she lost advantage, she'd be dead. Her fingers groped, and she discovered a wire running up the mech's back that sent an electric tingle up her arm. Grip tightening, she savagely yanked. The wire came free and the mechanical sagged, lifeless.

Fredek Fynn came running up, metal bar in his hand. He saw that Inyx had triumphed.

"Amazing," he said, admiration in his voice. "Few men ever best one of them in single combat. But where'd it come from? It just appeared in the middle of the nest."

"I got lucky stopping it." From his awestruck look she knew that wasn't a good-enough explanation. "Here, look," she told him. "It's not all that mysterious. This wire is

147

similar to our arteries. I dislodged it and the mech simply
. . . died.''

Fredek examined the ragged end of the copper strand.
He hesitantly touched it to the junction where it had been
attached. The mechanical jerked spastically but did not
come back to life.

"You've killed it," he said finally. "I'll tell the others
about this. It might give us a better chance."

"Any report from the scouts?" she asked.

"None. Knoton doesn't maintain a base. He moves
constantly through the maze."

"He knows it better than we do, that's for certain. This
attack proves it. Still, he needs somewhere to repair his
troops. I can't believe he doesn't have some fixed point for
a base." Inyx had become the leader of the nest more by
default than anything she'd actually done so far. She had
carefully mapped out all entrances to the large room and
had the more sane of her followers guard them. And still
the mech leader had infiltrated at least one—the deacti-
vated one at her feet—through their lines. Knoton had
either discovered a hidden passage or burrowed through
lines, silently killing more than a dozen human and near-
human hybrid guards.

"He might not have the need for rest that we do," said
the man. "To constantly explore increases his chances for
survival."

"He has a base," she said firmly. "And find out how
this one got into the nest. That worries me. Our security is
worthless unless we discover his route in."

The man began probing the walls nearby while Inyx
searched the fallen mech for any bit of information it
might yield. She found nothing, but Fredek did.

"The illusions we encounter from time to time aren't as
vivid for the mechs," said Fredek. "See this wall?" He
placed his hands flat against blank expanse.

"So?"

"Watch." Fredek's hands vanished to the wrists, to the

elbows. Curious, Inyx came to examine the section. Her questing hand vanished, too. While it appeared substantial enough, the wall wasn't actually there at all.

"Illusion," she said glumly.

"I've heard it said that the Twistings know if you are a sorcerer. If so, the illusions are more real, more numerous. Others, like me, see very few, and those are only basic images. Walls." Fredek Fynn's hand disappeared all the way to his wrist again.

"Does the Lord look into the Twistings?" she asked. "Perhaps that is the real source for the illusions."

Fredek shrugged.

"He," Inyx went on, "can meddle to his heart's content with those able to appreciate his illusions. The others he couldn't care less about. But this wall mirage is more basic than seeing monsters. It's been here since I entered the nest."

"No one has found it before."

"How can you tell?" she asked bitterly, looking around the nest. The human and hybrid food-gathering party had returned and were again engaging in their own personal madnesses. Some sang to themselves, others argued with thin air, and still others descended into catatonia. It wasn't a prepossessing army she led.

Fredek's hand rested lightly on her shoulder.

"If anyone can escape the Twistings, you are the one. There's something about you, Inyx, that won't let you stop. No matter what the Lord does, you'll escape."

"It's not the Lord I'm worried about at the moment. It's Knoton. The mechs have a much more organized band. Why haven't they killed all the humans by now?"

"We're tougher than we look. You might say some of us fight with insane fury."

"Where's the scouting party now? I'd like to know if they've located Knoton. This attack inside the nest means he's become bolder and may be ready to launch a big attack against us."

"Let's do some exploring on our own," said Fredek. He glanced at the spot in the wall where illusion plastered over the corridor.

"Just the two of us? That's risky." She wanted more than just Fredek to back her up before following this path. Knoton had known of it; an ambush might lay ahead. But Inyx was a realist. There weren't any humans or hybrids left in the nest she'd trust. Her ablest troops were scouting for the exit from the Twistings, for Knoton, for anything that might aid them. Inyx heaved a sigh and picked up her knife. "All right. Let's explore."

She closed her eyes and stepped forward. If she'd watched, there wasn't any way she could have walked so boldly through what appeared to be solid wall. As it was, she felt a light tingle on her face and then only cool air. She walked forward, knife point leading the way. The darkness enveloped her and forced the woman to rely on other senses she'd sharpened since entering the Twistings.

Inyx heard Fredek behind. To either side came the soft susurration of air caressing solid. Ahead—nothing. She advanced with a step, test, full-weight stride. While skirmishing with Knoton, she'd seen several of the mech's bodyguards vanish through the floor. The trap led downward. She'd tried to find the spot again after the fight but had failed. Either it had vanished or she'd gotten turned around in the maze and had not found the proper spot again.

In the Twistings, either was possible.

A rectangle of dim light showed ahead. She slowed her snail's pace even more and held out her arm to stop Fredek. Inyx spoke to him in a low voice.

"Back me up. I'm going to look. If anything happens, run for the nest and don't try to rescue me."

"Knoton's ahead, isn't he?"

"I can feel him," she said.

Inyx advanced, eyes fixed on the light. When she was twenty yards away from the doorway, she dropped to her belly and began crawling. She'd learned that the mechs' vision often failed to pick up slow-moving objects at floor level. Inyx vowed to be very slow-moving.

Rusty clanking noises greeted her. The voices of arguing mechanicals soon drowned out that sound. When she peeked around the door frame, she saw what she'd suspected existed and what no human had found. Knoton did have a base. He fostered the myth of constantly being on the move to give added protection. Dozens of mechs were in various stages of disassembly. This corresponded to a mechanical hospital where technicians worked to restore limbs and sight and mobility.

"Kill them. Kill them all!" raged Knoton.

Inyx sought out a pile of discarded metal parts and hid behind it. She then watched, unobserved.

"I counsel caution. This new human, this Inyx. We can deal with her."

"You're wrong, Kolommo. She is like the rest. The Lord is human; he casts us into this foul, deadly place. She is human. We can kill her in revenge."

"You," accused Kolommo, "seek only revenge. Knoton, she is right when she says we are all exiles together now with the same common enemy. If we worked as a single unit—"

"No!"

Knoton's vehemence made Inyx cringe. This Kolommo appeared to be the second in command. Ideas formed in Inyx's brain. Remove Knoton and deal with a more rational mechanical. It could be done. It had to be done, if any of them were to escape the Twistings.

She duck-walked back to the darkened corridor. On silent feet she rejoined Fredek. Motioning him back toward the nest, she hiked in silence until they emerged again in familiar territory.

"They have a base, don't they?" he demanded.

"They do. And I see a way to carry this fight to them. Whatever happens, we've got to take out Knoton. From then on—it might be easier for all of us."

Inyx went to plot strategy.

"The scouts are back," shouted Fredek. Inyx saw a small band—fewer in number than when it had left—tiredly walking down the main corridor leading into the nest. She rose and went to stand beside Fredek.

"What did you find?" she demanded of the party leader.

The smile greeting her made her wince. Three teeth had been knocked out recently, leaving bloody spaces in his mouth. But the smile was one of triumph.

"A room, some distance away, guarded by every maze creature we've ever seen and a few that are new to us."

"A guarded room? In the Twistings?" That by itself was curious. The entire maze was one giant locked room.

"We couldn't make much headway, but we did find the spot where the blue creatures are spawned."

He gestured to a woman lugging a large pack. Inside were dozens of small yellow fruits.

"They're cannibals," he explained with some distaste. "These are their eggs—or whatever you'd call them. Eventually they hatch into blue globs."

"And that's what they live on—that's what *we* live on," Inyx said.

"We learned how to decoy them, too. That's how we got these. We found a group of the cappers and chased them into the spawning area. That made the blue monsters spittin' angry. They came rushing out, jaws snappin' shut and chompin' down on anything and everything in sight." He stood, proud of his accomplishment. For all the years people had been exiled to the Twistings, this was the first real systematic exploration that had been done.

Inyx felt a curious combination of elation and emotional depression. The scouting party had found the single room in the Twistings that the Lord guarded with maze creatures and more. Further, she saw how to defeat Knoton and his mechanicals. But it would be bloody. Many would die, both human and mechanical, and in between.

"Can you get the monsters attacking down this corridor?" she asked, sketching out the location she meant. The quick nod convinced her the time had come.

One way or the other, the civil war in the Twistings would be over soon.

"Quiet," Inyx hissed. "They'll hear us." She sent the word back along the line of eager, kill-crazed humans slowly wending their way down the darkened corridor Fredek had discovered. Ahead gleamed the rectangle leading into Knoton's base camp and repair area. The coming battle would decide all.

"When do we fight?" demanded one of her less stable men. "I want to kill, kill, kill!"

"Soon," she soothed. "When we hear the blue globs attack them. Then we follow in." She wanted the maze creatures to do as much of the fighting as possible. Let Knoton fight them off; then, when the mech leader least expected it, she would attack.

Her ragtag band grew increasingly restive. They weren't used to discipline. When Inyx heard loud chomping sounds, she knew that they didn't have to wait any longer. Fredek and the scouts had decoyed the blue monsters into Knoton's camp. Now came the real fight.

"Forward!" she cried. The humans surged behind her, waving clubs made from mech legs and human thigh bones, makeshift knives, anything that swung or cut. They burst into Knoton's camp and found the metallic beings in disarray. The blue monsters had rampaged through, causing great destruction. Inyx hated to admit it, even to herself, but this carnage sickened her. These weren't flesh-and-blood creatures; they were the product of some mage or technician.

But they lived. They thought. They experienced life. Not as she knew it, but they sensed they were alive.

"There's the she-demon," shouted Knoton. "Kill her!"

Inyx advanced to lunge with her sword, the point severing the vital wire in one mech's back panel. She fought through toward Knoton, to see if she couldn't end this battle by eliminating the opposition leader, when she noticed that some of the mechs falling to her sword evaporated when they touched ground.

"Illusion!" she shouted to Fredek Fynn, just entering by way of the main corridor. "Not all's real."

While she didn't know for certain, Inyx guessed that the Lord of the Twistings had learned of what transpired in his grand maze. He personally controlled the illusions she now fought as hard as any real opponent. She pictured the Lord sitting in a chair, a smug expression on his face. He revelled in their misfortune. He sent wave after wave of illusion to torment and hurt and confuse. She remembered him clowning about. She remembered all too well the pain and humiliation she'd felt when placed in his tiny maze.

Inyx vowed then and there to kill him with her bare hands.

She fought like a dozen warriors.

Snakes coiled about her feet. She ignored them. Single-eyed giants attacked. She dodged out of their way. But the pain, the paralysis, the gut-wrenching sense of disorientation, those she couldn't simply deny. Inyx fought all the harder. The more pain he sent her, the more she hated the Lord of the Twistings.

In a way, that series of illusions and agonies gave her strength to continue.

"Call it off, Knoton," begged another mech. Inyx recognized the broad metal back as belonging to Kolommo. Knoton shoved the other out of the way.

"Stop!" cried Inyx, motioning wildly to Fredek. It was too late. Fredek Fynn swung a metal bar with ferocious strength. Kolommo's head exploded as if a death spell had focused on it. Inyx saw her only chance for peaceful alliance shattered into a million fragments.

"Murderer!" raged Knoton.

Inyx stumbled forward to stop the mechanical's attack on Fredek. A transparent barrier stopped her.

"No, Lord, don't do this. Let me through!" She pounded furiously on the clear wall to no avail. Inyx sagged, felt crushing despair, shook it off, and then turned and bolted for the corridor through which the humans had attacked. Down the darkened course she ran, into the now deserted nest, out and down another corridor. The last of the blue gobbling monsters waddled along, retreating from the fury of the mechanical counterattack.

She slashed at one before it sank deadly teeth into her body. Again, Inyx cut. The creature died. She forced her way over its blue bulk and into the hall beyond. The woman felt time slipping away. She sprinted, found the proper path and soon enough followed Fredek's route into Knoton's base.

Inyx saw the mechanical leader decapitate Fredek Fynn just as she entered.

Her body went numb. Her mind slipped out of synchronization with her actions. Inyx stumbled forward, her sword dangling from her shock-deadened fingers.

"You, human. You're next," Knoton said savagely. The mechanical charged, iron bar swinging with effortless ease above his head.

Inyx didn't quite snap out of her shock by the time Knoton came within attacking range. But the Lord didn't want his private showing to end too soon. The iron bar crashed into an invisible wall, reverberated, and bounced free of Knoton's hands. The mech stared in disbelief, then attacked with his bare hands.

The time between first and second assaults measured only seconds, but Inyx recovered enough to feel cold rage welling inside her. Fredek Fynn had been murdered by this monster. She could avenge the death—the real death. A mechanism didn't die. It simply stopped functioning. The woman could stop Knoton's functioning.

Her sword cut ended abruptly against Knoton's neck. The blade shattered like crystal on impact, but it drove the mech to his knees. Inyx followed up instantly, kicking, trying to smash the glass eyes and blind her opponent.

"It's not that easy, human," growled Knoton.

The words turned Inyx into a fighting machine. She hadn't asked to be placed in the Twistings. This metal monster had killed the only friend she'd found. And for what reason? Irrational hatred of flesh and blood. That was what drove Knoton.

All around them flowed unreality. Humans fought with mechs. Mechs and hybrids battled. And intermixed with all were the Lord of the Twistings' illusions. But to the dark-haired woman, only one thing mattered: Knoton.

Her fingers locked on cold metal flanges in deadly combat.

"Die!" he grunted, metal arms circling her body. Inyx allowed it, keeping her arms free of the grip. She had disabled one mech by loosening a wire in the back. Knoton would die, too.

She gasped as he tightened his grip around her body. The air gusted from her lungs. He tightened more, preventing her from sucking in new oxygen. Her fingers groped blindly, seeking out the vital conductor in the back. Just as the world spun and turned to blackness, she jerked free the wire.

Knoton roared and thrashed around—but he didn't collapse.

"Human," he said, backing away from her. "My body is different. That slows me, but it does not stop me." Inyx studied the way the mech moved. Ripping free the wire she'd found had done more than slow Knoton. His left leg dragged perceptibly.

She gasped until her lungs had enough air, then looked

around for a weapon. She'd learned her lesson; Knoton was far too strong for her. Nothing useful lay about.

Her eyes widened when she glanced over Knoton's shoulder. A wraith glided forward, tiny hands reaching out. Inyx didn't know if it was illusion or reality. One way meant advantage for her; the other meant lost concentration.

The wraith glided . . . through . . . Knoton. The mech took no notice. The Lord sent her illusion. However she responded, Inyx had betrayed herself to Knoton. He launched an attack, low and at her legs. He lifted her up and dropped her heavily to the floor. She looked up and saw metallic death descending toward her head.

Inyx jerked hard to the mech's left side. What little damage she'd caused saved her. Knoton tried to follow her motion, failed. The woman evaded his clumsy lunge and again faced him, this time with her sword again in hand.

Or was it?

Inyx tightened her grip. The pommel felt substantial, but she hadn't picked up the sword. It was illusion, but one Knoton saw.

"Knoton, let's talk. I know that Kolommo wanted a truce. We can come to an agreement."

"After you've destroyed my friend?"

"You killed mine, also." She didn't make the novice's mistake of looking toward the dead Fredek Fynn. Such an opening for Knoton would spell her death.

Knoton slowed, stopped. He took in all the sounds of battle. The illusion mixed with reality cost lives.

"We have a mutual enemy," she said. "The man who put us both into the Twistings. Let's fight the Lord, not each other."

"You fight well—for a human."

"You show compassion—for a mech."

They stood facing each other. Slowly the tension went out of the air. They abandoned their fighting stances.

"The only victor in this will be the Lord," said Knoton. "How do we end it?"

"We stop fighting. We join forces."

"No!"

"Then we just stop fighting."

Knoton and Inyx backed away from each other and slowly regained control of their forces. Knoton had the easier time of it, but Inyx soon persuaded her side to desist. The engagement broke off gradually, and each side assembled at a different part of the room. Bodies, both bone and metal, littered the floor. All over, illusion ended and a myriad corpses vanished into nothingness.

"Back to the nest," ordered Inyx.

Knoton stared at her from across the room. The civil war in the Twistings had ended—for the moment.

CHAPTER SIXTEEN

Lan Martak had to stop and use his healing spells once more on the shoulder wound. The mechanical's dart had become infected in spite of his earlier treatment. Lan sat and chanted the spell, feeling the magics soothe and begin the healing process anew. But as he relaxed after the pain finally began to recede, he also grew increasingly lethargic. Even at the best of times when he was uninjured, the use of magic sapped his strength quickly.

"Can we stay here for a while, Krek?"

"It is not a good place. I detect many of the mechanicals nearby." The spider bobbed up and down, talons grating against the walls and floor of the Twistings.

"Can't go on. So tired. Must sleep. Wish I had a bed. Wish I could just . . ." Lan drifted off to fitful sleep.

And awoke screaming.

Krek towered over him, peering down, concern in his soft chocolate-colored eyes.

"What is it?"

"M-my dreams. They turned all around like I was in a dark, rotating barrel. I felt as if I'd been impaled, but it was more than physical torture. The dreams were . . . rotted."

"The Lord of the Twistings sends those to you as his present," said the spider. "He wants to keep you from using your full powers. Distrust yourself and the spells you know will not work."

"I do need to keep my confidence," admitted Lan. He wiped some of the sweat from his forehead. His clothing had become thoroughly drenched while he slept and dreamed. "But if I can't sleep without experiencing more of that . . ." He shook his head.

The dreams—nightmares—had been horrific. What was worse, he found it difficult to separate the fantasy from the reality. It mattered little whether his eyes were open or shut. This hallway stretching forever in front of him played such an important part in his dream. Did that mean he had seen what would happen? Had the dream been a fore-shadowing? Did his powers now include prophecy?

"I don't want to walk along this corridor, Krek," he said, voice shaking. "Awful things will happen. The floors will grow teeth and swallow us. The walls will crush in. Everything will turn black and start to spin. The—"

"Lan Martak," snapped the arachnid. "Those were dreams. We face some illusion, yes. The Lord sends those to taunt you. But our own fear is the greatest obstacle. I know the location of the door leading out of the Twistings. Shall we go there and escape, or do you wish to cower here on the floor for the rest of your miserable existence?"

Such words from Krek took Lan by surprise. The man usually was on the giving end of lectures like that.

"The maze, Krek. I've *seen*."

"You have seen nothing. The Lord of the Twistings puts it all into your thick skull. Once there, it can never escape. That much is obvious. I grow tired of this place. There are no juicy grubs to eat, no fit places to hang a web, no peaks to scale. It is not a proper place for a Webmaster. Not at all.''

"Which way is out?" Lan asked. As he stood, vertigo assailed him. He felt as if he were being turned inside out. But he struggled to keep moving, in spite of the feeling of falling, turning, going in all the wrong directions. He had to rely on Krek's inbred sense rather than on his own distorted ones.

The spider trooped off, talons clicking merrily on the floor. Lan followed more slowly. The wound, his tiredness, the feeling of *something* about to happen made him uneasy.

Every step produced more giddiness and disorientation.

"Stop, Krek, wait. Are you sure you know where we're going?"

"Yes."

Illusions flittered just at the periphery of Lan's vision. He concentrated on them and noted how they vanished when he uttered certain ward spells. But this constant magic use drained his vitality further. When the Lord of the Twistings appeared behind him, he had nothing left to draw on.

"So good, yes, you're much better than I thought," crowed the Lord.

"Friend Lan Martak, he is here," said Krek. The spider turned in the narrow corridor and faced the Lord. "This is no illusion."

"Can you be so sure, fuzz-legs?" taunted the Lord. "I control this maze perfectly. The Twistings are mine, all mine! I love them, I do!"

"He is here, Lan Martak. Kill him. Or get out of my way and allow me to do so!"

Lan wobbled. What was real, what wasn't? Krek seemed sure the Lord had actually come into the treacherous maze personally. Lan guessed differently. This was illusion.

"He only mocks us, Krek. He can cast his images wherever he wants."

"No image, this. I smell, I sense, I see. The vibrations are those of a living man. The Lord of the Twistings can die here and now." The spider lurched over Lan, mandibles clacking. They slashed through the air just inches in front of the Lord. He never flinched.

The man—the image?—danced back, saying, "Can you be so sure? Lan is the mage. He knows about such things. You know about grubs. Like these."

Wrist-thick grubs poked their blunt, blind heads out of newly formed tunnels drilled through the walls. Lan blinked twice. He sensed their ghostly, insubstantial nature, yet still felt the presence of another human. Krek might be right about this actually being the Lord of the Twistings, in the flesh.

"Kill him, Krek. You're right. It is the Lord."

"Yes, Krek, kill me," taunted the man in the fool's outfit. He rolled and somersaulted backward down the hall. "Who knows, you might be the next Lord of the Twistings. What a sight. A giant spider ruling over the Twistings."

Krek launched himself in a shallow attack, mandibles aiming for the legs. The Lord leaped, dodged, and retreated.

"Very good. But you can do better."

Lan pulled out the death tube and fired past Krek's bulk. The lightning blast singed the spider's legs—but the effect on the Lord was startling. Rage contorted his face. He clenched his hands into tight fists and screamed.

"A barrier," said Krek. "He has constructed one of the magical barriers between us."

Lan felt the barrier being erected but had been powerless to stop it. The Lord had somehow sensed the impending danger—or had the spell ready in case Krek got too close. However it had happened, the transparent wall had saved the Lord from fiery death.

The Lord of the Twistings vanished from sight, as if he had been an illusion. With him went the barrier.

"The walls are not as substantial as they seem," commented Krek. "We are not too near our entry point into the Twistings. Perhaps there are more ways in and out of the maze."

"Let's get to the room as fast as we can. I feel like I'm going to pass out."

"That explains your cavalier use of that fire-thrower. You almost set my legs on fire." The spider shuddered. "I urge you to be more careful in the future."

"I will. Now, hurry."

Krek lumbered along in the opposite direction, taking turns and finding corridors where Lan didn't think any were possible. When he had decided to tell Krek they walked in circles, they entered the small room that had been their first sight in the Twistings.

"Peculiar," observed Krek. "Note the way these pots burn for no reason." Black kettles filled with flowers of sulfur dangled over small fires. The released odor gave the room a hint of hell.

"He's a showman. He knows how to stage and upstage. The sulfur keeps everyone off their guard until his spells turn them around. By the time the magic wears off, the people have wandered blindly into the maze and are irretrievably lost."

"I found my way back easily enough."

"Maybe he's never tackled anyone of your . . . size," Lan finished lamely.

"True. I am somewhat larger than most on this world. You humans are not very big. Which can be a good thing. There are so many of you, as is. The crowding conditions would be brutal if all of you were my size." The spider shuddered, adding, "What an ugly thought."

Lan stopped listening to his friend and went to examine the inner workings of the vault door. His fingers pressed into the cold silver metal. Due to his weakness, Lan had difficulty turning his magics inward, to the mechanism operating the toggles. His magical senses reached out, lightly touched, failed to find.

He sank to his knees, head resting against the door.

"Can't do it," he said, almost crying. "There's something inside. A spell, a magic. But I can't get a feel for it. If only I could manipulate it, the door would open."

"It is not purely mechanical?" asked Krek. The spider walked forward and spread four powerful legs out, engulfing the door. Talons dug into the rim of the door. He pushed. Lan watched as tendons stood out when the spider's muscles contracted with gargantuan effort. A faint metal tearing noise came, but no movement of the vault door. Krek worked harder, then relaxed.

"It is beyond me, totally beyond the limits of my feeble strength. Oh, I've grown too weak being away from my dear Egrii Mountains. Why did I ever leave, why do I torture myself by roaming? Dear little Klawn, my hatchlings, I left them all, and for what? This!"

"There, there, Krek. We both tried and couldn't move this metallic mountain."

"Try your flame spell. Melt it down!"

"Wouldn't work. I can barely walk. That requires intense concentration. I need to rest, to regain my strength. Maybe then we can get out. But I wonder . . ."

Lan Martak had felt enervated during the confrontation with the Lord of the Twistings in the corridor, but the nearer they came to the vault room, the weaker he seemed. It was as if some power drained him mentally and physically. He struggled to sit up and work his powers to detect any use of magic. That had been his first and most potent ability: sensing magic. Nothing impinged on his mind.

That didn't mean spells weren't in use around him, though. He had found subtle magics, clever spells, ones so sublime his untrained skills failed to detect them. Such might be the case now.

"Lan Martak, sounds of battle come from down the corridor."

He strained and heard human voices.

"We can't get out this way, not right now. Don't let the

Twistings confuse you, Krek. Remember how to get back here, and let's go see if we can help.''

"Help?" the spider said, gusting a baleful sigh. "A shopworn human and a lonely spider far from mountainous home and loving family? How can we help anyone when we fail so completely to help ourselves? Oh, very well. Let us be off."

Lan managed to walk unassisted. He noted that strength returned as he put more and more distance between himself and the vault room. The man filed this information away for future investigation. He'd missed the use of a spell against him, of that he was sure. By the time they reached a juncture in the interminable corridors, he felt strong enough to use the knife.

Which was a good thing. A waddling blue glob engaged Krek, and three wraiths silently glided up to attack Lan's left flank. He struck out with his fist and sent one wraith fluttering back. He lunged with his knife and skewered the second. Red blood cascaded down a purple front. The third wraith threw him entirely off balance; Lan kicked at it, and his foot sailed through its insubstantial form—illusion.

The blue monster rolled over in the corridor and waddled off in the opposite direction, Krek chasing. Lan tried to stop his friend. Splitting forces wasn't smart. But he had his hands full with the three wraiths, two real, one illusion. What made his effort even harder was the way the illusory creature kept changing color. Purple and purple attacked. He stabbed and a new fountain of blood squirted forth. The other wasn't there, except in his mind.

The battle shifted in his favor. One wraith finally lay dead, the other severely wounded. The illusion hovered nearby, then winked out of existence.

"Lan Martak, come quickly!" rang out Krek's agitated request. "We are needed!"

The man followed Krek's pathway through the maze easily. The spider had severely wounded the blue glob. Droplets of thick, ichorous blood marked the corridors taken. He exploded into a hall where three humans and a part-human and part-mech hybrid fought against one of the blue monsters. Even as he watched, one of the men slipped; the powerful jaws opened and closed on an arm.

"Aieee!" screeched Krek, leaping over the battling humans. Lan followed, keeping the humans from attacking Krek.

"He fights like a thousand men," marvelled one.

"That he does," said Lan. "Follow him. We can finish off the blue thing and let him rest."

"Who are you?" demanded one of the women. Her eyes narrowed in suspicion. "You are not of the nest."

"No, I guess not. My friend and I have just been cast into the maze."

"The Lord exiles more and more," said another woman sadly. "I wish I could leave."

"We know where the entry point to the Twistings is," said Lan. "When we rest up a bit, we can all go and tackle it. We can get out of this damnable maze and stop the Lord."

"You *are* freshly arrived," said the hybrid. A mechanical arm scratched a battered, scraggly-bearded human face. "Doesn't he sound a lot like her?"

"He does, at that," answered one of the women.

"Her? Who do you mean?"

"Our leader. She has come into the Twistings, found our nest, and even battled Knoton to a truce. For the first time in any of our memories, we fight only the maze creatures instead of each other."

"Yes," piped up another. "With the mechanicals on our side—or not opposing us—we hope to live much longer."

"Some leader," Lan said admiringly.

"That she is. Inyx is quite a woman."

"Inyx!" he cried. "Inyx is your leader? Take me to her at once. Now!"

"Well . . ."

"At once! Krek, we've found Inyx."

The spider sauntered up, blood dripping from his furry legs.

"Good. I tire of this slaughter. Those blue balls begin to annoy me, and intelligent conversation with Inyx again would do much to lift my sagging spirits."

The small band of humans, hybrid, and spider hastened off in search of the nest—and Inyx.

At last, Lan Martak had found her.

CHAPTER SEVENTEEN

"Inyx!" he exclaimed. "We've found you at last."

Inyx looked up, perplexed. The voice sounded familiar, but who could it be down here in the Twistings?

She looked up, blinked as if her eyes deceived her, then said, "Lan? It's really you! Oh, Lan!"

They rushed forward and flung eager arms around one another. They clung to each other for long minutes, then both began to babble at the same time.

"How'd you get—"

"Why didn't you—"

"Are you really the leader—"

"*Silence!*" bellowed Krek. The echoes deafened all in the nest. Absolute quiet fell as Krek carefully folded his legs and sat down in the center of the room. All eyes followed his every movement. When he had reached a comfortable position, he said, "Now you may continue. But please do not carry on like that. Speak in complete sentences. I try to tell my hatchlings communication is important. Granted, the hatchlings are more intelligent than humans, but—"

"Krek!" Inyx threw her arms around his nearest leg

and squeezed, pressing her face against the coppery fur.

"You are getting my leg wet," he said, but the complaint carried no sting. In a lower voice, he added, "I am glad to see you also, Inyx. You have no idea how dull it has been travelling with him."

Lan shook his head in wonderment. Dull? Of all the words to describe their travels, dull was far down on his list.

"Tell us how you came to be the leader of this . . . army." Lan looked around at the dozens of dirty faces, the demented smiles, the vacant stares.

Inyx took a deep breath and began her story, finishing with ". . . and Knoton and I fought it out to a tie. We've got an uneasy alliance now. He doesn't trust humans, and I don't trust him. But for the first time in anyone's memory the mechanicals aren't systematically killing the humans and hybrids."

"That's progress," said Lan. "Maybe we can muster enough support to attack in force through the entry point. Krek remembers the way back. The disorientation we felt on entering the Twistings didn't affect him. I don't think the Lord was expecting such a different set of senses."

"We can't leave, not yet," she said. "Did you notice any spell holding you within the maze?"

"I felt weaker at the vault door," he admitted.

"A part of Claybore's body is within the maze."

"We know. We overheard Claybore and Alberto Silvain talking about it."

"Silvain," she hissed. With effort, Inyx pushed him from her mind and continued. "My scouts have found a guarded room. That is very unusual in this place."

"The entire Twistings is a prison," mused Lan. "So, with Knoton's help, we get into this guarded room, destroy whatever part of Claybore we find, *then* leave."

"Can you destroy anything of Claybore's?" she asked. "I had the impression he was invulnerable."

He quickly explained all he and Krek had learned about how a far greater mage named Terrill had dismembered the sorcerer and spread his parts along the Cenotaph Road.

"Claybore can't be destroyed, but his powers are vastly weaker than when his body is reassembled."

"Weaker," she muttered in disbelief. "Can you destroy whatever it is of Claybore's?" she repeated. "You don't have the magical skills of this Terrill."

"He is growing more and more adept," spoke up Krek. "Lan Martak is not master mage, but his abilities far exceed those of when you were last in our company."

"With a few of the spells in this," Lan said, pulling out and tapping his leather-bound grimoire, "I can destroy—I think. If not, then neutralizing might be the next best thing. It's not going to be easy, and I need to rest up." He winced as Inyx's hand rested on his injured shoulder. "But we can come through it."

Their eyes locked and unspoken communication flowed. They'd triumph because they were together. At last.

"I drove them out," said Inyx, "when I found out they actually were cannibals. I wasn't going to let them live off the others. They really worried me the way they skulked around."

"You couldn't sleep too soundly yourself," said Lan. "If I'd known that they were stalking around in the maze, I'm not sure I could have slept at all."

"You've not been sleeping too well, anyway," the woman pointed out. "Are your nightmares getting worse? Last night you screamed aloud, and never woke up."

Lan tried to calm his heart as it raced away. Last night's dreams had been the worst yet. He didn't know if the Lord triggered the dreams or if it indicated some change within himself. He'd started receiving them when he and Claybore had faced one another on the way to the summit of Mount Tartanius. The sorcerer had sent the frightening, evil visions in hopes of scaring Lan away. If anything, however, the dreams then helped strengthen his growing powers.

Now he felt only debilitated by the dreams. He couldn't fight. His dream-self tried forming spells, fighting back, evading. Nothing worked. The maze worked its insidious power on him and left him as weak as a newborn kitten.

"Fredek once said that only those used to magic were affected inside the Twistings. Maybe he was right."

"Fredek?"

"He's dead. Knoton killed him." From the tone of her voice Lan knew that this Fredek had meant something to her. Irrational jealousy flared, then went away, dying down into something more manageable.

"I've thought of you often," he said softly.

"And I of you, Lan. In the whiteness between worlds I had little else to do but think. One place was the same as another. And in here . . ." She held out her hands palms up and looked around. There wasn't all that much to do or see.

He started to ask about Fredek, then stopped. It wasn't any of his business. Krek lumbered into the nest and relieved him of the burden of finding some other, safer topic.

"Friend Inyx, Lan Martak, good news. I have worked my way through to the guarded room. It is not difficult to reach, but it is protected in ways that perplex me."

"Simple frontal assault won't work, is that what you're saying, old spider?"

"Just that. In addition to the more obvious ploys, like falling weights, razor-edged flooring panels, and the maze creatures, the Lord of the Twistings has added many traps similar to those we crossed on our way into his palace."

"What kind of traps?" asked Inyx.

"I don't know how he rigs them," admitted Lan. "Most magic spells require considerable energy to form and maintain. Over a span of hours or weeks, perhaps even years, the binding spells fade and become inoperative. The

Lord has contrived spells that are mechanically activated. I assume they'd last as long as the mechanical triggering device did.''

''They produce partial paralysis or intense pain,'' said Inyx, remembering her bout in one of the Lord's other mazes.

''How'd you know?'' asked Lan.

''I owe the Lord much. When we get out of the Twistings, he shall be repaid in full for all he's done to me—and the others.''

Lan looked at her and tried to penetrate the depths of her anger. He felt cold inside when he realized exactly how intense her feelings were concerning the Lord. Here was something else he didn't care to explore any further.

''I think the Lord watches me more carefully than you,'' said Lan, ''because I know some magic. What this Fredek said holds true, at least in my case. Why don't you and Krek go ahead and scout around this room while I bring up the rear?''

''Good,'' said Inyx. She and Krek left, Lan following at a respectable distance. He felt the flow of magic whirling about him. Whether or not the Lord actually watched—and Lan thought he did—the magics at work meant he'd have to be constantly alert. His few spells seemed pitiful in comparison to those a full-fledged mage commanded, but they were all he had. They'd have to serve him well.

An hour hiking through the maze got Lan totally turned around and lost. He felt the subtle tuggings of spells at every junction. Once, he attempted to alter the magic and found he didn't have nearly enough power. A basic part of the Twistings was contained in those mysterious guard-spells, he thought. Pass through an intersection, be just a bit more turned around by the spell. They operated directly on the brain and caused disorientation.

Krek didn't appear to be the least affected. His nervous system, his brain, body, everything, worked differently from a human's. Lan found himself wondering how these spells affected the mechanicals. They, too, experienced the twisting effect coming into the maze. He'd spoken with several of the hybrids while he convalesced, and they'd told similar stories.

"Here, friend Inyx," came the spider's voice. Lan stopped fifty feet away to avoid attracting magics until Inyx had personally examined the room containing a body part of Claybore's.

"Lan, come ahead. We need something more than eyes now," echoed her voice. He hastened to join them.

The room lacked a door, but Lan "felt" the intense magics sparking to and fro in place of a solid barrier. Strewn out at random along the corridor in either direction he "saw" the dull glowing pates where the Lord's traps waited for the unwary.

"I wonder how many times one of those traps can be triggered," he thought aloud.

"Shall I test it and see?" asked Krek.

"No, let's wait a few minutes. I doubt we're going to be allowed to examine the room without picking up some company." The words were hardly out of his mouth when one of the globular blue maze creatures waddled into view, mouth opening and closing with loud clacking sounds. It walked over several of the traps without ill effect.

"I shall dispatch it," offered Krek. Lan waved the spider ahead, wanting to get on with a closer examination of the room. While the spider chased off the blue monster, Lan ran hands along the wall. He didn't know what he sought, but when his hands vanished to the wrists through an illusory wall panel, he knew he'd found it.

"Let's go in and see what we can find," he told Inyx. The pair walked through the wall into darkness.

"Lan," she said, reaching out and touching his shoulder. He winced slightly. In the week or so since he'd received the injury from the mechanical's dart, it had mostly healed but remained tender. "Sorry," she said. "I get spooked in places like this."

"You should," he said in a low voice. He "saw" things she never could. Looking out of the walls were glowing eyes, opening mouths filled with dagger-sharp teeth, groping hands. He avoided them; they seemed frozen into their positions inside the walls. A clever choosing of a path meant safety. Lan led the woman through to a small anteroom free of striving creatures and obvious traps.

"I don't want to leave," said Inyx. "I . . . I want to stay here forever."

"I feel it, too. Strong. So very strong." Lan closed his eyes and concentrated. Filling his mind like warm, sudsy water came the spell. It frothed and boiled about his thoughts, soothing and changing them. Why leave the Twistings? This place was so nice. *Don't leave, never leave,* came the repeated, insistent command.

"Lan, let's get out of here. Now. I don't want to, but I know we shouldn't stay any longer."

Lan fought the tide welling up, managed to push it away. He chanted a control spell that held away and momentarily contained the urgings coming from the room.

"We're so close," he said. "Just a bit further down this corridor. We can see what's in the room. I can hold it back. I know it."

"Lan, please."

He saw the strained look on her face. He nodded, took her hand, and led her back through the groping hands and staring eyes of the creatures imprisoned in the wall. Once, in his haste to depart, he came too close to one of the beasts. It almost cost him his life.

Tiny hands with improbable strength grabbed his arm and pulled him powerfully into the wall. He slammed hard, the impact jolting him. Teeth slashed at his shoulder. Intense pain flared as the wall creature bit and gnawed at his flesh. As long as the tiny hands held him, he wasn't going to escape.

"Lan, what's wrong?" demanded Inyx.

"Go find Krek," he told her. "Hurry!" She moved past

and exited the illusory wall panel. Never had Lan felt more
alone, abandoned. But he had to hang on, fight, strive.

He pulled forth his dagger and awkwardly stabbed at the
wall. His blade turned aside and left a deep scratch. The
creature was so intent on devouring him it didn't even feel
the mark. He tried to cut the hands off at the wrists; no
luck.

Teeth dug even deeper into his upper arm and shoulder.

To panic now meant death. He tried to reach around for
the death tube, but it had been pinned between his body
and the wall; he had no way of freeing it. There had to be
another way to escape. There had to be!

He used the pain as a focal point for his power. The
number of spells he had even halfway mastered was small,
but Lan knew how to select with care. The fire spell was
the most familiar to him. In spite of brutally sharp teeth
ripping his flesh, he summoned up the energy he needed,
moulded it, held it in place with the magical chants, then
shoved his free palm against the wall.

A cascade of fire fell from his fingertips. A lightning
bolt lashed out of his palm. The wall creature slackened its
attack. Again Lan Martak sent forth his flaming punishment.
And again and again.

He weakened from the effort of casting the spell. Like
water flowing out a hole in the bottom of a jug, his
strength ran away. When he was sure that the hands
gripping him would hold him till he died, he heard Krek's
bellow just a few feet away.

"Lan Martak, do not play these hide-and-seek games.
Come here immediately. The maze creatures congregate
too quickly for us to fight them off."

One last surge of energy from deep inside sent sputter-
ing blue sparks dancing along his fingers. Somehow, this
was enough. The creature trapped inside the wall released
him. Lan stumbled forward, through the wall, and onto his
face in front of Krek.

"You need not abase yourself when I call," said the

spider in a testy voice. "Departure is more important than obeisance."

"My arm, shoulder," he said weakly. But on examination he found no wounds, not even a bloody scratch. Lan sat and stupidly checked himself again. "All illusion," he finally said. "All that inside was pure illusion. Remarkable."

"I am not as prone to believing unreality as you, friend Lan Martak. I do, however, see a good bit of reality which I cannot fight."

Lan rose to his feet and felt some of his strength returning. The cappers and blue eating monsters had been joined by other, stranger beasts. Lan had to agree with the spider. This wasn't the healthiest place in the world to be right now.

The trio left, the waddling blue appetites following along behind them.

"Let's take another couple days before we go in," said Lan. "I'll be back to normal by then."

"Why didn't you tell me something had grabbed you?" Inyx stamped her foot down solidly. "I was frightened in the dark, yes, but not so much you had to send me away like a small child."

"You saw my wounds—or lack of them. What grabbed me was pure illusion, but one my mind accepted as real. I felt it, couldn't escape its clutches, was terrified of it. I'm not so sure I know how to stop it, even after looking through the grimoire. This," he said, tapping the small brown leather-covered book, "contains much information, but it can't tell everything I might encounter."

"The walls were filled with clutching hands," said Inyx, her eyes distant, as if she focused on those creatures. She sat down beside Lan and shivered. "How horrible."

"We've been through worse, you and I."

"Being apart was bad enough," she said. "But the way we're forced apart is worse."

"I know about Luister len-Larrotti," he said. "Something

similar happened to me, but it was much more pleasant.''
Lan remembered the times in the Suzerain of Melitarsus'
mansion. He'd been imprisoned both magically and
physically, but the bonds were less damaging for him than
Inyx's had been for her.

She turned blue eyes to look into his brown ones. In the
nest there was neither day nor night, only a perpetual
twilight. But most of the people slept now, preparing for
the assault on the room. For the span of several heartbeats,
Inyx and Lan said nothing.

He took her in his arms and pulled her closer. Their
mouths brushed lightly, then the kiss deepened into passion.
All they'd been through kindled their need for one another
into a raging desire.

"Lan, I—"

"No talk," he said. "This is the time for action." His
mouth crushed into hers again, this time with lips slightly
parted. Tongues lightly collided, danced about, then began
erotically caressing.

Their hands moved and unwanted clothing vanished as if
by magic. The only magic was in their need for one
another.

Lan cupped one of Inyx's breasts and felt the life pulsat-
ing within her body. No matter where they touched one
another, what they did, it fed their passions and pushed
them to a fever pitch.

For a moment, Inyx stiffened and held him away. The
memory of Luister len-Larrotti still haunted her. She'd
been used, abused, turned into a slave and a whore. Then
she relaxed and urged Lan on. With him it was different.
She did as she desired, not as another dictated.

Locked together, they surged and peaked, then lay side
by side, arms circling one another's sweaty body.

"It's been a long time since I've *wanted* to make love,"
she said. "Since Reinhardt." She shuddered as she said
that. Len-Larrotti had used that image to hold her; the
power of her husband's memory had been shattered forever.

She remembered him fondly now, but she could go on.
She had gained the strength to go on.

"Tired?" Lan asked.

"Yes. It's been a hectic day and this . . ." She sighed
deeply and snuggled closer. "It took the last of my energy."

"Are you sure?" he asked, his fingers lightly tracing
patterns over her naked flesh. Everywhere he touched
tingled and glowed. Lan used the spell for cheating
weakness. Like all spells, it had its drawbacks. The energy
they both got would leave them even more drained after
the effects wore off.

It seemed like a good tradeoff to Lan.

And to Inyx.

CHAPTER EIGHTEEN

"This hidden corridor is the real entry point to the room," said Lan, sketching the approach for the benefit of the others. "The doorway appears open, but the spells guarding it are incredibly active. I don't even want to think about trying to go through that way."

"How do you know these things?" demanded Knoton. "How will our gaining entry into this particular room aid any of us to escape the Twistings?"

He faced the mechanical leader. In subtle ways emotion played across that metallic visage. Lan wished he knew what those mirrored emotions meant.

"You wish to leave this maze, right? We—the humans and hybrids—will help you do that, but first we have to destroy what's in the room. We're being held inside the Twistings by its power. Destroy it, destroy that magical hold. Only then can we truly combine forces and break out of the maze."

"The mechanicals feel its pull also," he admitted reluctantly. "You can destroy this fetish if we gain entry?"

"I'll be truthful about it. I think I might be able to. I'm no sorcerer, but I control certain spells. I've been practicing the one required to rob the fetish, as you call it, of its power. We might able to destroy it then. But I can't promise that. What I can promise is that controlling whatever we find in that room will give a big edge in helping us escape.''

"Why?" The mechanical still appeared skeptical.

"The Lord of the Twistings' power resides in that room. The grey-clad soldiers obey him because of what he holds there. Remove it, or threaten it enough, and the Lord must respond. Only with such an opening can we act.''

"We mechs will not be used as shock troops. We will not bear the brunt of the fighting.''

"It's going to be an equal opportunity for all to die,'' said Inyx. "Lan, Krek, and I have scouted this place. Just looking draws the maze creatures. *All* of them.''

"Even the ones from deeper levels.'' Knoton didn't appear happy with this prospect.

Lan decided not to pursue this line of inquiry. He hadn't known there were deeper levels to the Twistings. That fact didn't make it any easier—or harder—accomplishing his mission.

"We're agreed, then?" he asked. "We cooperate? All of us?"

"You lead?" asked Knoton. The mechanical obviously had reservations. He respected Inyx and her fighting ability, but that didn't mean trust went with it. This interloper fresh to the Twistings presented an even riskier proposition.

"I will. I can 'see' the traps in the floors. The maze creatures don't trigger them; we do. The magics guarding the room are potent. I can lead a small party through the hidden corridor. From there, we get into unknown territory. This is all the further Inyx and I reached.'' Lan paused, then added, "With your help, Knoton, we can break through and crush the Lord's power.''

"For five years I've roamed the Twistings,'' said the mechanical. "For five long years I've built my hatred for the Lord. This is the first real opportunity to vent it. I shall follow—but cautiously."

"You and Inyx can work out the details," said Lan. The woman nodded assent. She and Knoton had a working relationship that he and Krek didn't have with the mechanical. And Lan Martak wanted one more night's sleep, even sleep troubled by nightmares, before again confronting the magics guarding that single room.

He'd have been better off staying awake. The nightmare quality of his dreams gave him little rest.

"My men mark the way," said Knoton in an accusing tone. He wanted Lan to know that they wouldn't be led into the maze and left helpless and confused as to direction.

"It won't do much good," said Lan. "I tried doing that when I first entered the Twistings. Only Krek seems to have the knack for finding his way around. The magics don't work as effectively on him."

One of the mechs trotted back and spoke quietly to Knoton. Knoton shook his fist.

"What you say is correct. The markings vanish even as we make them. It is not this way in other parts of the maze."

"The Lord most carefully protects this area," said Krek. "We are not too distant from where we encountered him. I believe he keeps whatever it is in this room because of easy access. If he needs to recover it quickly, there is not far to go."

"There won't be any treachery on our part, Knoton," Inyx told the mechanical. "We risk just as much as you in this."

"I wish that I could believe humans."

"Not all of us are like the Lord."

"Enough are," he said sullenly.

Lan stopped and thrust out his arms to stop the party's progress. He'd "seen" one of the patches of floor glowing a dull amber. The other traps had been marked with different colors. This one was not only at a variance, it hadn't been here when he, Krek, and Inyx had passed before.

"What is it?" demanded Knoton. The mech held his steel rod firmly in one hand, ready for any challenge.

"New traps. The Lord's expecting us."

"I see nothing. Push on!"

"Wait!" But Lan failed to hold back the mechs' leader. Knoton stepped squarely into the center of the patch.

He let out a shriek as the floor dissolved under him. Only Lan's quick reflexes saved the mechanical from plunging downward into a vat of slowly boiling acid. Still, Lan's reaction availed them little when his hands slowly slipped on the rod both gripped. Knoton struggled, dangling by this steel lifeline.

"Inyx, help me. I can't hang on much longer. He's heavy!"

Whirring sounds from above told Lan everything was going to be all right. Krek spun a hunting web. It rocketed down and stuck to the mechanical's body. But when the spider began pulling up, the web-stuff slid free of Knoton's body.

"The acid prevents a good hold. The mist from the boiling vat wets Knoton all over."

"Can't hang on much longer," grunted Lan. His muscles knotted painfully from the strain. The droplets of acid billowing up in a misty cloud stung his hands, his arms, threatened his face and eyes. He heaved, jockeyed for position, felt himself slipping.

"Let go," said the mechanical. "Save yourself."

"We're in this together, dammit," muttered Lan. He started chanting the revitalization spell, even though its success now would prevent him from being very effective later.

Krek bobbed past him. All eight legs gripped the mech's head. Through some spiderish lore Lan knew nothing about, Krek went back up the strand, lugging Knoton behind. Only when Lan heard a heavy metallic thud signalling the mech's safety did he relax.

His wrist muscles knotted on him, half-closing his hand with reaction. He sat and chanted a minor healing spell.

The muscles relaxed. He hadn't used much of his reservoir of strength.

"How'd you do that, Krek?" he asked. "You said the acid made it impossible to pull Knoton up."

"My hunting web refused to stick. I held him in my talons."

"He dented the sides," said the mech, sitting across the trap door and shaking his battered, talon-marked head. "And I want to thank you all for saving me."

"Next time believe me when I say there's trouble ahead."

"Lan, hurry. The maze creatures are forming." Inyx clubbed at one with the blunted tip of her sword. The capper recoiled, hands grabbing for her blade. She kicked at precisely the right instant to send it stumbling back into the pack of its allies.

"Drop a plank across this trap," Knoton ordered one of his lieutenants. "Then give us protection when we reach the room." The mechanical snapped a salute and hurried off to obey.

Lan jumped over the opened trap and joined Inyx and Krek in stabbing and slashing at a few of the cappers. When one of the blue monsters blundered into the same corridor, the cappers turned their attention to it and vanished, almost as if they had been real ghosts. For once, the avariciousness of the maze creatures aided Lan and the others.

"Disabling trap here, no way of telling what that one is over there," he said as he walked. The glowing squares had tripled in number, and the colors were subtly altered. Once, a mechanical blundered across a patch Lan saw as light green. The concussion from the explosion knocked them to their knees. Knoton received another heavy dent in his head when flying debris from the destroyed mech rebounded with a loud twang. -

"The Lord has certainly prepared the way for us," said Inyx. "It's a good thing you're able to see them, Lan. No one could possibly get in, otherwise."

"I'm afraid we may have some trouble of our own," he

replied. The maze creatures blocked their path—and the beasts weren't hindered by triggering the traps.

"Stay still for a moment," said Lan. He concentrated, trying to figure out the difference between the maze monsters and the humans: why should one trigger the traps while the other did not?

The creatures attacked. Lan raised his hand and a blinding sheet of fire swept forth. The reaction startled all of them. The traps in the floor erupted with a cornucopia of violences. Sonic waves, metallic spear points, spells that ruptured the cells of the body, spells turning bone to ash, all these decimated the attacking monsters. For a moment, the surviving beasts stood, as if confused, then turned and fled. Lan shot forth another radiant plane of energy; again came the virulent destruction.

"What did you do?" asked Knoton, astounded.

"Most of those traps are triggered by body heat. Krek doesn't trip them because his body is too far off the ground. Those creatures must have slower metabolisms than humans."

"But I triggered the trap back in the other corridor," protested Knoton. "My body temperature is very low."

"That was a mechanical trap," pointed out Lan. "Your weight set it off. I told you it 'looked' different. Somehow, the Lord has used magics to create these traps. Different ones give off different colors. What I see as amber must be purely physical nastiness. The other colors represent a coding of magical spells. Even some of them must be physically activated." All too well he remembered the sight of the mech being blown apart.

"Friend Lan Martak, what you say is probably true. It is not good policy to stand about idly talking it over, especially if the Lord of the Twistings listens in."

"You're right, Krek. Quick, time it now. We're almost to the doorway."

The small group stopped in front of the room. Lan hurriedly scanned it and felt mounting disappointment.

The spells guarding the door had been strengthened—doubled. The thought of again going down that gauntlet behind the false panel in the wall made him sick to his stomach. The faces embedded in the walls, the tiny groping hands, the teeth, always the teeth . . .

To enter the room required that they again reach the relatively safe anteroom at the end of the hidden corridor.

"No way in here. To go through that door is instant death."

"There's nothing to worry about," said Knoton. "In," he commanded one of his troops. The mechanical bravely walked forward. Lan had to reach out and restrain Inyx to keep her from following and attempting to stop the mech.

"See?" said Knoton proudly when his mechanical had entered the room. "There's nothing to worry over. You live too much in magics, human. You see them everywhere, even where they are not. I can . . ."

Knoton's words trailed off when he saw the delayed reaction inside the room. The mechanical he'd sent in slowly wavered, as if seen through intense heat. Losing all rigidity, the doomed mech began to puddle and flow. When only a pool remained on the floor, a dull pop sounded. Steam clouded the scene for a moment, then those still outside could again see into the room.

"He's gone," said Knoton in a low voice. "He melted down into slag and vanished."

"The spells aren't obvious ones," said Lan. "I have no idea what most of them do, but that's only a start. The reaction is postponed long enough to lure in others. It's a wonder this single trap hasn't eradicated all the maze monsters."

"He's gone," repeated Knoton, staring into the space where he'd sent the mech to its destruction. "Again, I misjudged you, human. You do care about our safety."

"And you're misjudging me now," said Lan. "I'm going to ask you to follow your friend in."

"What? And perish in such a fashion as that?" Knoton's eyes flared red and green and amber in his fury.

"Maybe. It's a distinct possibility, one that can't be discounted totally. I hope it won't come to that, but we've got to go in. Krek's too big. Besides, we need him outside to stand off the maze creatures. You and Inyx and me—we go in."

"What of my troops?"

"I need help, not an entire army. Too many will distract me and increase the danger. I can warn you and Inyx in time. To relay that along a line . . ." Lan shrugged.

"I see. What am I to do?"

"Follow us," spoke up Inyx. "We've been down this corridor before, but couldn't get all the way in. This time we have to. I doubt the Lord will give us a third chance."

Lan located the illusory wall panel. He took several deep breaths to calm himself. Walking the path between the inner walls took all of his courage when he knew what awaited him if he stepped too far either left or right. Hands. Teeth. Pain, intense pain, pain so excruciating he almost felt it before it began.

"Don't look to either side," he cautioned, then went forward. Lan fancied grabbing hands missed him by fractions of an inch. He moved slowly, studying their footing, finding a few new traps. Once he even "felt" an overhead trap. Knoton disabled the trigger device, showing exceptional dexterity in the cramped quarters. Finally the trio reached the "safe" spot attained on the last excursion.

The tiny room hadn't changed in any detail. Either the Lord of the Twistings thought they'd never reach this far or his protective spells inside the anteroom were superior to those they avoided reaching this point. Lan studied the floor, the wall, the ceiling.

"Through that door is the way into the other room—the one we can see from the hallway where Krek waits."

"Won't we set off the same spell if we enter?"

"We've come in the back way. I'd bet the Lord himself follows this path in when he wants whatever is out there."

"Let's get on with it, Lan," urged Inyx. "I feel that time is against us."

"You're right." He settled his thoughts, worked up the controls needed for his deadliest spells, then entered the room.

Lan Martak froze inside when he saw the face staring at him. Bright, malevolent eyes peered forth from under beetle brows. Dark hair swept back to expose a high forehead. Ears several times too big stuck out like jug handles on either side.

And the head rested on a pedestal.

"It's like Claybore has been decapitated again," Inyx said in a voice hardly above a whisper.

"Such evil. Look at it," marvelled Lan. "Terrill skinned Claybore in addition to dismembering him. This is the flesh flayed off Claybore's skull. The skull and eyes beneath this are artificial—the flesh is all Claybore's. I feel the power radiating from it like heat from a blast furnace."

"I feel it, also," said Knoton.

"And I. This is what holds us in the maze? *This?*" Inyx walked around the marble pedestal studying the grisly sight. "Only the flesh from the sorcerer's skull exerts magical power enough to keep us in the Twistings?"

"Every part of Claybore is potent," explained Lan. "Even the skin from his face."

"But it seems so minor!" protested the woman. She drew her sword and started to slash at the head.

"Wait," said Knoton, holding her arm and preventing the stroke. "Wait for what Lan Martak has to say."

"Hmmm, oh, thanks, Knoton. You're right. Destroying it physically isn't possible. It must be done magically." Lan's attention drifted from the others and back to the spell Abasi-Abi had spent much of his lifetime perfecting. If a truly major portion of Claybore's body had been found, Lan doubted the spell would have worked, that he had the expertise to cast it. But for such a minor bodily artifact, he thought he might be successful.

He took the leather-bound grimoire and chanted the complex spell repeatedly. All around him rose a shimmering curtain of energy, cutting him off from the others, making him an island unto himself. This battle had to be fought alone, using weapons he scarcely comprehended. A dead sorcerer's spell turned against a living, disembodied sorcerer's flesh—and Lan Martak was the agent delivering the potent magical energies.

He controlled and guided immense flows. At first he thought he failed. He kept on, persisting until sweat flowed in thick rivers down his face. Lan never once wiped away the perspiration. His concentration had to be perfect, his chanting impeccable.

"It's changing shape," cried Inyx. "Keep on, Lan. You're doing it!"

Lan Martak scarcely heard her. He had caught a tiny thread, teased it, pulled on it. This led him to a slightly larger string, then to a cable. He tugged harder and harder until elation mounted inside.

"Almost there. Almost have it. Almost oh, yes, there!"

The potent spells locked in Claybore's facial skin vanished, but in that instant of dissipation a gateway between worlds opened.

Lan Martak faced the fleshless skull and limbless torso of Claybore, master mage and would-be conqueror.

"You've ruined my face, worm. My face is destroyed! So shall yours be!" The deep eye sockets clouded over, then boiled with the turbulence of ruby death. The beams shone forth directly at Lan, but he had encountered these before and lived. The beams deflected from his body. Behind, he heard the very walls of the Twistings begin to sizzle and burn.

"This is only the beginning, Claybore," said Lan in slow, measured tones. "I failed miserably when you regained your body. No longer. Your face is gone forever. So shall your tongue go."

"My tongue?" The death beams winked out. "How do you know about that?"

Lan allowed the control spells he held to weaken. The gateway between him and Claybore vanished. It was a pathetic gesture, this taunting of the sorcerer, but it was all Lan could do. At the moment.

"Are you all right?" asked Knoton, hurrying to the human's side. Strong metals arms supported Lan.

"All right? I'm great!"

"You destroyed it, Lan. The skin is gone. Nothing but ash left. And even more important, the geas holding us inside the Twistings is lifted. I can't feel it anymore."

"Yes, it's gone," he agreed. Weakly, he cast forth magical tendrils, seeking out the Lord of the Twistings' spells. Most had vanished. "And the Lord knows what has happened. He underestimated us. He thought his minor traps and the maze creatures would stop us. He's lost!"

"Come along, then. Let's find the entry point and put a real end to him," declared Knoton.

"He's mine," said Inyx.

"I want him," Lan said.

"We can argue over it on our way out. Free!" screamed Knoton. "We are free of the Twistings!"

Lan indicated one of the giant holes blasted through the wall by Claybore's ruby death beam. They climbed through to rejoin Krek and the others. Lan felt elated at his victory; he also felt as if every bone in his body had turned to water.

"Help me, Inyx," he said. "Otherwise, I'll fall flat on my face."

"If you do, we go together," she said.

They hurried off to the entry point, following Knoton and his mechanicals.

CHAPTER NINETEEN

"Slow down, Knoton," called out Lan. "I can't keep up."

"Don't worry about him," said Inyx. "He senses release from the Twistings. He's been trapped here for five years—and I think he might be guessing wrong. There's never anything to indicate the passage of time."

"Knoton's time sense is accurate. He runs an internal clock," said Krek. "An admirable ability, always knowing what time it is. Though what use it would be to a mountain arachnid, I cannot say offhand. We swing so freely, the breezes gently caressing our furry legs, swinging us in our webs. Ah, yes, how I long for those days. It will be good to escape this infernal underground."

"Krek," said Lan. "Stop the mechanicals. There might be traps ahead they can't detect."

"Nothing stands between them and freedom now."

Lan still worried. The destruction of Claybore's face had lifted the geas holding them in the maze. Obviously, the longer in the Twistings, the more powerful the spell became on an individual. That also meant the urge to flee, once the geas lifted, would be greater in those who'd been the longest in the maze world.

"Up ahead. There is the entry point, friend Lan Martak."

Lan cursed his weakness from so much magic use, but there wasn't anything he could do now but rest and recoup his energy. He felt as if he'd been battered and beaten by Claybore's entire grey legion. Magic required a different set of responses, ones he still had great difficulty controlling.

"No!" came the anguished shriek from inside the room.

Lan momentarily forgot his tiredness and sprinted forward, outdistancing both Inyx and Krek. Inside the room, metallic fists pounding on the vault door, stood Knoton.

"It won't open. We can't make it open."

Lan closed his eyes and cast forth his magical senses. What he encountered only added to his tiredness. He sank to the floor, sitting cross-legged.

"It's worse than you think, Knoton," he said. "The Lord has permanently sealed the vault door. The spells operating it have been cancelled and, as if that's not enough, he has ordered his technicians to weld it shut. Feel the heat seeping through? No amount of work on our part will open this way again."

"Trapped for eternity," wailed the mechanical.

"Perhaps not," spoke up Krek. "The Lord of the Twistings entered once to taunt us. He vanished in a part of the maze some little distance from this point. This might indicate another entrance—and a potential exit. After all, he hardly expected to go to the room containing Claybore's skin by traversing his own maze."

Lan snapped his head up and around to stare at the spider. His brain refused to think. Exhaustion poured into his body like melted tar. But the spider was right.

"We did think he vanished too quickly to ever reach this room," he said. "And the Lord wouldn't want to go through so much of the maze to get to his precious skin down in the room where we just were. He's got an entrance other than this one! He has to!''

''And one leading to his playroom,'' said Inyx. ''I'd bet on it. He dotes on the smaller man-trap mazes he keeps there. He seldom leaves that damned room, but when he does, I'll bet he comes down into the Twistings to gloat over his fine creations.''

''Let's go do some wall tapping,'' suggested Lan. He got to his feet, legs almost refusing to support his weight. Going to the forlorn Knoton, he put an arm around the cool metal shoulder and said, ''We're beaten—this round. Next one will be ours.''

The pair left the sealed vault door behind, never looking back.

''The scouts have worked the entire area,'' said Inyx, ''and they've not found a single hidden corridor or room.''

''It's there,'' said Lan. ''I know it. The Lord isn't the kind to have only one way out of his hidey-hole.''

Knoton clanked in and propped himself against a wall. His left leg still dragged slightly, and there hadn't been time to fix the dents in his head caused by Krek's talons. The mechanical had seen better days.

''We found a hidden room,'' he said without preamble.

''What? Where?'' demanded Lan. ''Show me.''

''A word first with you—and Inyx.''

Lan and the woman exchanged quick glances. This was unexpected. They knew the mech wanted out, and this might be the path. Why stand around and discuss anything?

''We are on the brink of escape,'' said Knoton. ''When you destroyed the facial skin of this sorcerer, you told me that we would decide who got to kill the Lord of the Twistings. I want him. That is my condition for aiding you and telling where this room is in the maze.''

''Do you hate him so?'' asked Lan. ''He's cast you in, yes, but you'd keep us in the Twistings just for revenge?''

''Humans are treacherous,'' snapped Knoton. Softening

his tone a little he said, "I am sorry. You have shown yourselves to be honorable. This is something I do not expect out of nonmechanical life forms."

"Humph," sniffed Krek. The spider turned away, already miffed at the turn the conversation took.

"I have as much claim on him," said Inyx. "What he did to me was insane. He must be punished."

"We all have good claim against him, but you're forgetting something. Even after we're out of the Twistings, there's an entire army to contend with. We have to assume Claybore still supports him. While the skin is gone, the entire world remains a plump-enough prize. Unless I miss my guess, Alberto Silvain is no fool. He'll defend the Lord ably." Lan sat back, arms crossed on his chest. "When we escape, it must be one convulsive burst outward, with force. We have to convince Silvain that the Lord is no longer in control, that the object he seeks for his master is already destroyed."

"Silvain would never fight for the Lord without the promise of recovering Claybore's skin," said Inyx, sureness in her voice. "You're right, Lan. Convince Silvain and he will not fight for the Lord. He'd kill the Lord in an instant. But he's another one I want: Alberto Silvain."

"Let's come to a quick agreement that we'd all love to see all these men punished. After we're out, we might even be in control. If so, we can discuss the matter further, at leisure when we can look at this from many different perspectives. But let's first get out of the Twistings."

"Agreed," said Inyx. She looked to Knoton. The mechanical hesitated, then gave a quick head nod.

"To this room you've found. May it lead us right up into the center of the Lord's palace!"

"It's a relatively simple spell," Lan explained. "I'm not going to have any trouble at all with it."

"But?" asked Inyx. "You're hesitating. That's not like you, Lan."

"I don't know what we'll find on the other side. The grey-clad soldiers still support the Lord. I'd feel better if we had some sort of cat's-paw to shove through ahead of us."

"Like the maze creatures?" piped up Krek. "I have noticed them following us. Their voracity has not diminished one iota since the geas was lifted. If anything, they become bolder."

"Can you herd them into this room?"

"Of course," answered the spider. He lumbered off to begin assembling the cappers, blue monsters, and others.

"Stand back. This might be dangerous." Lan chanted his spells and felt the wards diminish before him. In less than a minute the last of the spells collapsed.

The way into the Lord of the Twistings' palace opened to them.

"I was right!" exclaimed Inyx. "That's his playroom." She peered around the edge of the doorway, obviously eager to go through and find the man who had imprisoned them all in the Twistings.

"Hey-yahhhh!" came the cry from the corridor. Knoton, Lan, and Inyx jumped back in time to avoid being crushed under the waddling might of dozens of the blue eating creatures. They yammered, jaws snapping, and charged forth into the Lord's playroom. Behind came a legion of cappers, drifting along, tiny hands wiggling in front. And behind them, mandibles clashing together in order to keep the herd moving in the proper direction, rolled Krek.

"That ought to soften up the opposition," said Lan. "Knoton, get your troops together. We've got a ruler to depose!"

Lan turned to find Inyx, but the dark-haired woman had already left the Twistings. He hurried after, death tube in hand. The device had grown progressively weaker after each usage, and Lan worried that it might fail him now. Still, it provided a better weapon than his dagger.

"Inyx!" he called. "Where are you?" He listened and

heard sounds of battle coming from the next room. The man tried to re-create the floor plan of the palace; he thought the noise came from the audience chamber. He hurried to find out.

The enormous room had been filled with the voracious maze creatures. Finding more food than they had had during their entire existence in the Twistings, the beasts devoured unsuspecting soldiers and dismembered slow-moving mechanicals. The soldiers fought half-heartedly, wanting more to run than fight. Lan didn't blame them. Such carnage wasn't seen often, even on the most hard-won of human battlefields. After all, humans don't stop to eat their victims.

"Away!" came a familiar voice. "Away, back to the Twistings!" The words carried more than a demand; magics laced them, as well. Lan even hesitated on hearing the command, feeling the spell's power, wanting to return. Then he got a better grip on himself. He was exhausted, but he wasn't beaten into the ground.

Lan homed in on the Lord. The man stood in the center of the large stage, arms upraised, head tossed back, imploring the powers to drive away the hordes wrecking his audience chamber. A quick vault brought Lan onto the stage. The Lord lowered his gaze, staring directly into Lan's eyes. There was no sign of recognition.

"Why do you do this to me?" the ruler asked, his voice hurt and childlike.

"You don't recognize these creatures? They live in the Twistings. And the humans, the mechanicals, the hybrids? Those are people you exiled."

"I don't understand."

But Lan did. The man played for time. He felt the stirrings of magical powers all around. He immediately began building counterspells, but the Lord had the edge. Years of practice, years of malevolence, had honed his powers to an edge sharper than Lan's newly acquired ability. When the Lord unleashed his magics, Lan staggered under the onslaught—but he held his position.

Fighting a defensive battle, he maintained his composure. The Lord had failed to destroy him or push him back. This added to Lan's confidence. While the battle of magics tired him quickly, he thought he might soon break down the other's barriers.

"Die, you scum!" Lan heard from the side. He allowed his eyes to flicker over. Inyx held death tubes in both hands. The weapons flared and smashed into the Lord's defensive barrier. With this added assault, the man couldn't continue.

Wordlessly, he spun and vanished behind curtains at the side of the stage. Inyx followed him with her death tubes, setting fire to the curtains. But the Lord of the Twistings had fled.

"Inyx, wait," cried Lan. He stumbled forward. "He knows the palace too well. There are traps everywhere."

"He's mine, dammit!" the woman flared. "After what he did to me in that damned maze, dammit, he's mine!"

Lan turned and surveyed the room. The Lord's mechanicals had put up no resistance whatsoever when they saw Knoton. If anything, the sight had provided a rallying point for them to rebel. Only Claybore's soldiers fought those pouring out of the maze—and the battle went poorly for them.

Taken by surprise, unable to fight off the blue monsters and cappers, the soldiers quickly retreated. Only one pocket of resistance formed. Lan figured this was commanded by one of the higher-ranking officers, perhaps even Alberto Silvain.

"The Lord's not going anywhere. He'll not lose all he's built here. Let's eliminate the grey-clads, then go after him. There's still Silvain to think about."

"But the Lord . . ." Inyx glared at the spot where the Lord of the Twistings had disappeared, then she slumped. "You're right. Following him now is too dangerous. Wipe out the others, get control, *then* root him out like the worm that he is.''

Krek tottered up to the edge of the stage and looked Lan squarely in the eye.

The arachnid said, ''The maze creatures return to the Twistings. I do not understand it.''

''The Lord cast a spell ordering them to go back. I felt it and managed to fight it off before it grew too strong. He underestimated us again. He won't do it anymore.''

''The battle goes against him,'' observed the spider. ''His mechanicals rally to Knoton. The soldiers are all but eliminated. Do you wish to assist removing one last group of them?''

''Let's go,'' Lan urged, his arm around Inyx's waist. He tightened the grip slightly to move her along. He didn't want her running off alone in search of the Lord. He'd never asked what the man had done to her; it had to be awful. She'd discussed her stay at Luister len-Larrotti's with him but positively refused to do more than proclaim her hatred for the Lord of the Twistings and vow she'd personally kill him.

He'd touched her in ways too deep for her to speak of.

The man's evil would end—soon.

''There, over there!'' called Knoton. He stood at the front of a tight band of mechs. They held death tubes and other weapons picked up from fallen humans. Lan felt the buzz of concern surge through their ranks as he and Inyx joined the metallic leader. The other mechanicals weren't sure of any humans. One quick gesture from Knoton quieted them.

''The greys are behind that wall,'' said Knoton. ''A frontal assault will be deadly for us.''

''The room is small. There can't be more than a few dozen inside,'' said Inyx. ''They'll be in each other's way constantly.''

''Too bad the maze creatures returned,'' said Knoton. ''We could have used them.''

Lan said nothing while Inyx and Knoton discussed possible ways of attacking the soldiers' position. He paced and studied, his magical sense probing out. The man hesitated to use a spell against the soldiers for a variety of reasons. It drained him casting even the simplest of spells, but even more to the point was the Lord. Magics turned against their user were more devastating than any other kind; the mage had little in the way of defense against a spell personally conjured. Lan Martak didn't doubt for an instant that the Lord waited for him to make a mistake using a powerful spell.

He, more than any other single factor, had been responsible for the Lord's empire crumbling. Without his magical sense Claybore's body artifact wouldn't have been destroyed; the geas that formed the Lord's power core in the Twistings had been permanently removed from the struggle. Oh, yes, definitely, the Lord would be waiting for him to make a mistake.

"Use your cylinders against that part of the wall," Lan ordered. The mechanicals stared at him, then at one another. He was a human, no matter that Knoton tacitly approved of his continued life, and not to be trusted. "Do it. Now!" he roared.

The snap in his voice caused many to lift their weapons and fire. As the lightning cracks of energy smashed into the wall, Lan stepped back and waited. Less than five seconds elapsed before the wall fell in, exposing the soldiers.

"Krek," he said softly. "Ask the soldiers to surrender. Use your loudest voice."

The spider obeyed. His voice thundered forth. The sight of the tall mountain arachnid did much to demoralize the soldiers. Whether this was illusion or reality made no difference.

"Surrender!" Krek bellowed. And the soldiers quietly surrendered.

Inyx came to Lan and put her arm around him. He shook in reaction to the anticlimactic battle. The army of mechanicals surged forward and took prisoners rather than leaving corpses. Their reason for slaughter had been circumvented.

"Knoton?" called Lan. The set of the mech leader's head told him all he needed to know.

Alberto Silvain had not been in the room. And the Lord of the Twistings remained free in the palace. This battle had been relatively bloodless. The one to come—with Silvain and the Lord—wouldn't be carried off so easily.

He sagged and let Inyx help him to a chair for some well-deserved rest.

CHAPTER TWENTY

"A cenotaph opens," said Krek. "Very near. I feel it."

"So do I," said Lan. "And it just closed. I don't think Silvain escaped through it. I didn't have any 'feel' of it being used to move from this world to another."

"There are others nearby," the spider pointed out. "I cannot tell when they will activate."

"Let's not worry about that," Inyx said with feeling. "I want Alberto Silvain, but I want the Lord of the Twistings even more."

Lan Martak closed his eyes and let his senses tell him where the Lord was. The grey-clads had mostly surrendered. The few pockets of resistance faded as more and more of the mechanicals and others of the palace staff joined the battle. Word of the revolt would soon spread to the city and bring about unforeseen consequences. Lan had no idea how the populace of Dicca might respond to having their elected leader overthrown. After all, the Lord did deliver first-quality illusions, and the people of this city lived for their fantasy.

Still, a civil war raged outside. He'd seen rebel howlers

battling against the greys. That meant support for this palace revolt existed.

"He's returned to his playroom, as you called it, Inyx. He is working spells I can't begin to understand, but they are potent ones." Lan opened his eyes and twisted his head so that he could see Krek. Human and spider locked gazes for a moment. Krek finally bobbed his head in silent, reluctant agreement that he would do as Lan wished.

"I'll take him now," the woman declared. She hefted both of the death tubes and started for the room. Inyx hadn't gone five paces before a silken strand of web tangled her feet. She turned, sat down hard. An unbelieving look on her face, the dark-haired woman started to protest. Another gout of web-stuff circled her at the shoulders, pinning her arms to her sides. Still another closed off any protests.

"I do not like this, friend Lan Martak," complained the spider.

"It's got to be done. She wouldn't stand for a second against him. Not with the spells he's conjuring."

"Do you need my aid?"

"Thanks, old spider. This is one battle that has to be fought alone." Lan walked off, trying not to look at Inyx. He failed in this. He went to her, whispered in her ear. "He's a mage. I'm the only one here who has the slightest chance of defeating him." He kissed her. Inyx's eyes glared hot and blue at him.

It didn't make walking into the playroom any easier.

Lan had never felt more alone. Tired from his exertions in the Twistings, he barely held on to the control spells he needed for forging his defenses, his attacks. Krek and Inyx had to remain behind; in the battle he dared not have them in danger. The Lord would use them against him if at all possible. He had to maintain complete concentration, without worry for his friends' safety, or he would definitely fail.

But he was tired, so tired. Exhaustion worked on his

body as if he carried a ton of lead. Even the shoulder that
had sustained the mechanical's dart ached, and that wound
had long since healed.

"Don't make this any harder," he called out. "Surrender.
Let the citizens elect a new Lord of the Twistings."

"A new Lord?" came the hysterical reply. "A new
one? *I'm* the only Lord they need. I give them all the
illusion their small minds can handle. I present epics for
their amusements. I keep them happy. Why should they
replace me?"

"The Twistings is no more. Your political prison is
gone. I might be able to keep the mechanicals from killing
you, though why I should try is beyond me. Maybe it's
because you're human, too."

"Human? I'm more than human. I'm Lord!"

Lan edged into the room. The cubes of mazes filled
almost every possible area, the path between them forming
a maze of its own. Lan peered into the glass cubes as he
penetrated further into the Lord's last bastion. Tiny people
stared out, imploring, sobbing. They knew that their freedom depended on the outcome of this magical battle. They
knew Lan wanted their freedom.

Lan's mouth turned dry from nerves. The air felt moist
about him, almost as if he walked on an ocean bottom. As
he moved, it changed until he felt as if he swam through a
sponge. The denseness meant a spell working against him—
and one he didn't understand. His hand rested lightly on
the leather-bound grimoire he'd been given. To have had
time to master the spells in it! To have mastered just a
few . . .

"You are the one who released them from the Twistings.
How did you do it? Why did you do it?"

"You know why." Lan moved through the room until
he came to one wall. He guessed the Lord stayed near his
newest concoctions, possibly drawing power from those
mazes holding trapped humanity. "Claybore wants to take

over every world along the Cenotaph Road. He's caused me enough grief that I have to oppose him."

"But the Twistings!"

"Your artifact generating the geas holding everyone inside the maze was a part of Claybore at one time. Destroying it prevents him from ever regaining his full power."

Lan saw the Lord now. The man had changed into the fool's costume. He cavorted and danced along one edge of a maze. Clutched to his chest was a pale blue book.

"This is my finest maze," said the Lord. He sat on the edge of the cube, legs dangling and kicking. "And this is the plan for it. Oh, it is a good plan, too. I am astounded at my own brilliance. There are ever so many unique features inside."

Had he gone over the edge into total insanity? Or was this some ploy to lull Lan into thinking him harmless?

It didn't matter. For what he had caused, the endless agony, the untold misery, he had to die. Insane or not, he had to be stopped from further treachery.

Lan's fire spell welled up, ran down the length of his arms, exploded from fingertips. The fat blue sparks arced forth to touch the Lord. Nothing happened. Lan built the energy again, this time releasing a titanic bolt of energy that should have destroyed half the palace. Nothing. The Lord turned, eyes wide and innocent, as if seeing Lan for the first time.

"Why do you want to hurt me?" he asked.

The power he controlled was immense, and Lan felt his own powers weakening perceptibly.

"Give up to Knoton and the others," said Lan. His voice trembled from the strain. If the fire spell didn't work, he had to try another. But what?

The answer was given to him. Defense. The Lord laid down the book of blueprints and clapped his hands. Lan was driven to his knees by the pile-driver force hitting him. He turned his full attention to defense, erecting a protective barrier of his own. Blow after blow smashed into his body. He tried to deflect the force, to deny it, to counter it. All attempts failed. He felt as if he were being turned into a jellyfish. Joints snapped and bones almost broke.

Lan staggered forward. He had to stop the Lord. Now.

"Why don't you try out my brand-new maze? It's a very clever one. Oh, yes, so very clever. Come, enter."

Lan screamed as a powerful force swept him up and off his feet. He fell heavily beside the Lord, pinned down as if a dozen men sat on his chest. Then he began to sink through the surface of the cube. Watching, he saw the Lord grow in apparent size; he was being reduced and thrust into the cubic maze.

"Yes, it is a nice maze. I have it all here. The only way to escape is written down in these plans. And they are very, very clever, oh so complex. I don't even remember them all myself. Which is why I keep them written down." The Lord of the Twistings cackled demonically.

And Lan experienced real pain.

Every fiber of his body was pulled and strained to the utmost. It was as if he had been crushed in the jaws of a vise and jerked apart at the same time. He rolled, trying to dodge the red agony mounting inside and threatening to overwhelm him.

As quickly as the pain had begun, it stopped. Gasping, on hands and knees, sweat pouring in rivers to puddle on the transparent floor, he tried to regain his senses.

"That was merely the first trap set in my maze. There are others, ever so much nicer. Do trigger one of them. I wish to see how effective they are."

Lan looked up. He felt as if he'd aged a hundred years in a few minutes. Without even casting any of his spells, he knew it was impossible to escape. The barriers between him and the Lord were enormous. He was caught forever in another maze.

"You're not playing with me. I don't like that."

The trapped man discovered what that displeasure could bring. Not more pain. Fear. Gut-wrenching fear. He shrieked and clawed at slick glass walls. Everything he'd ever been frightened of in his life came to him. The dark, soul-crushing absolute dark. Tight, closed-in places. Slithering noises coming up behind him. Blindness. Helplessness. He couldn't see and he was trapped in a tight little box. Buried alive. Worms gnawing on his vitals, crawling through the empty sockets where his eyes had been. He clawed at his face, felt the flesh strip off under bloodied fingernails.

He screamed until he was hoarse. And still he felt fear. Until the Lord paralyzed his legs.

Lan fell forward, sobbing. The fear had vanished, but he was no longer able to walk.

"These are just a few of the wonders awaiting you. Explore my maze. There are some parts inside I'm not even sure about. Those were potent spells, very potent. I may have created something even I can't predict. Oh, isn't this wonderful?"

The Lord paced along the top of the cube, looking like a giant. At his feet, similarly huge, lay the book containing the operative spells. For Lan, an ocean might have separated him from the book. He could read the opened pages clearly—the printed letters were each larger than his hand. It did him no good.

"I may seal you inside permanently. Wouldn't that be nice? This is a special cube, oh, yes, very special. Time has no meaning in it. The stasis is one reason I have no clear idea what some of the spells actually do. This is ever so exciting."

Lan held on to his panic. He doubted the Lord's words about this being a stasis. Time flowed smoothly and at the same pace inside and out. Hearing the Lord's words and comprehending them proved that. Hearing the Lord and Inyx's voices . . .

"Inyx!" he cried, struggling to sit up. "Stay away!"

He heard her voice; he doubted she heard his—or would

heed his warnings. She had come after the Lord, somehow escaping the silken bonds Krek had spun for her. Lan tried to warn her away, to tell her to run. All in vain. Now she, too, would join him in an eternity of misery running the glassy corridors of this sadistic maze.

He looked up and saw two lightning spurts from death tubes strike the Lord. The sorcerer brushed such petty weapons aside.

"Come, join your friend in my maze," the Lord greeted. "Come. No, don't run. Don't!"

The Lord jumped down from the six-foot-high cube and pursued the woman. Lan flipped himself over, legs still paralyzed. But his eyes were keen and he read slowly through the spell in the book opened over his head. He studied it, puzzling over the strange terms. Then he realized the importance of the spell. The Lord had dropped the book face down and it had fallen open to the first page— the spell opening the maze cube was his.

Lan began chanting slowly, trying to master the spell. In the back of his mind he saw the Lord capturing Inyx, thrusting her into another of the mazes, torturing her, performing obscene acts on her. He had to use all the discipline he'd learned to ignore those images. They were his imagination, not reality.

He chanted faster. The syllables of the spell meant more to him. He struggled to sit up; the paralysis held him too firmly. He chanted faster, meaning almost his. Then the pieces of the spell came together in his mind. It was as if he had thrust a key into a lock and turned it.

The maze opened.

For a split second.

Lan laughed and cried in despair and hope. He'd been unable to keep the entry point open, but something as good as his escape had occurred. The spell book had fallen in and lay not a body's length away. Painfully crawling, he used fingernails to claw into the slick glassy material. Progress was slow, too slow.

What was happening in the room outside? Had the Lord caught Inyx? Lan Martak began uttering the strength-granting spells he had been taught by Abasi-Abi. He felt power flood into his body. The energy would last only a short while. Then he would collapse, possibly pass out, from the exertion.

Reaching the spell book controlling this maze, Lan hurriedly riffled through the pages. The Lord had entered them in a very logical order; he may have been insane, but that didn't prevent him from exhibiting impeccable logic. Lan studied, muttered the chants, got a feel for what must be done.

"No!" came the female cry from outside. The Lord had captured Inyx. "You carrion eater! I'd spend a lifetime in the Twistings before—" The rest of Inyx's words were cut off.

Composure came upon the trapped man like water rising around his head. He immersed himself totally in the spell book.

He gasped, staggered, and fell off the edge of the cube.

Free!

Free and past the point of exhaustion. Lan Martak had gotten out of the maze only to find himself on the verge of blacking out.

"How did you escape?" demanded the Lord. He held a struggling Inyx with careless ease in one hand. Lan felt the magics that allowed this feat. The woman fought with the fury of a hundred trapped tigers. "Ah, yes, I see it now. Oh, you are a clever one. Yes, very clever. I see I'll have to conjure open the maze again. This time you'll both go in. Won't that be nice, having a friend with you? And I suspect she's more than a friend." He sniggered as he bent to pick up the fallen spell book controlling the maze.

With contemptuous ease, the Lord picked up Lan and tossed him back onto the top of the maze. He dragged Inyx up and flung her down beside Lan. Lan gasped when he felt the ponderous weight descend on both of them, again holding them trapped.

"Now I can start anew with my opening spell. It *is* a complex one, too. Never can quite get it straight. Ah, yes, here it is."

The low, deep-throated chant began. Lan shook in impotent rage when he felt the hard surface of the maze cube begin to soften. In seconds he and Inyx would be cast into a pit worse than anything they'd encountered in the Twistings.

"It's open. And in you two go. Yes, in you goooooooo!"

Lan watched in fascinated horror as the Lord tossed up his hands and lost his balance. He fell heavily, then slipped into the maze where he had intended imprisoning them. Lan gasped when the crushing weight left his chest.

"What happened?" he sobbed out. The Lord's tiny face just inches away—and on the other side of the barrier—stared up in terror. "Why'd he slip like that?"

"Humans are not as sure-footed as we mountain arachnids," came Krek's calm voice. "I have said that repeatedly: eight legs are far better than two."

Lan saw a weighty strand of web-stuff dangling over the edge of the cube. Krek had spat forth a gobbet, which had struck the Lord, unbalanced him, and cast him into the hell he'd created for others. Below, through the barrier, Lan saw the Lord blunder into the pain trap. No sound came. None was necessary to know the vicious, biting pain the man experienced.

"He said that time was meaningless in this maze," said Inyx, her voice a monotone. "Is that true?"

"I can't say. Knowing his habits, I suspect that whoever's trapped in the maze is immortal. In a way, that's putting time in a bottle, a way of making time cease flowing." The Lord pushed past the pain trap and found a paralysis point embedded in a wall. His left arm hung limp. The panic on his face mounted.

"I'd better get him out," said Lan. "He's gone through enough."

"He's not gone through enough. Nor will he for centuries to come," said Inyx in that same shocky, emotionless voice. Lan sat up and saw that the woman held one of the death tubes.

"You can't reach him with that. The magic barriers forming this maze are impenetrable to physical attacks. Only one spell unlocks the entry point."

"Good." This single word came laden with emotions: hatred, glee, triumph.

Inyx turned the death tube from the tiny, struggling figure in the maze and pointed it directly at the blue book laying on the maze surface. She fired. The spell book disintegrated. Not even ash remained behind.

"Y-you just trapped him forever," Lan gasped out. "I can't conjure the spells to release him. No one can!"

"Let's find Alberto Silvain," she said. "He's the only unfinished business I have on this world."

Lan Martak didn't argue. He could barely stand.

CHAPTER TWENTY-ONE

"Where is he?" Inyx demanded of Knoton. "Where is Silvain?"

"The human leader of the grey soldiers?" If metal shoulders could have shrugged, Knoton's would have done so. "I have patrols out looking into every room of the palace. If he is within the walls, he'll be found. We look most of all for the Lord."

Lan Martak limped in and sat heavily. The way Knoton stared at him told the man how bad he actually looked. He felt worse. If someone had reached inside and ripped his heart out, he couldn't have been in a more debilitated state. The use of magic had pushed him beyond the limits of his endurance. Being cast into the Lord's maze had almost killed him. And now he had to perform one last task: finding Alberto Silvain.

"The Lord isn't a concern any longer. He will never again trouble you." The mechanical seemed inclined to doubt. Lan was too tired to argue. "But Silvain is another matter. He poses even more of a threat."

"Impossible."

"With Claybore backing him, the threat is incalculable,"

continued Lan. He fought blacking out, wondered if it were worth the effort not slipping into darkness and sweet oblivion. "Claybore conquers entire worlds. As he regains his body's parts and reconstructs himself, his power grows. The Lord of the Twistings was a powerful mage. He blended magic with the mechanical wondrously well, but Claybore is more powerful. He controls energies we cannot begin to comprehend." Darkness came over him. Lan succumbed to the warmth of that embrace.

When he awoke, he heard Inyx and Knoton arguing.

"Silvain is mine," the woman shouted. "I took care of the Lord. I want Silvain, too. He robbed me."

"Robbed you? Of what?" asked the mechanical.

"Revenge! I was going to kill Luister len-Larrotti for all the humiliation he gave me. Silvain killed him first. For that, if nothing of the other crimes he's committed, I want to see him skewered on the tip of my knife!"

"This world is returning to laws," said the mech. "Real trials, not the mock ones the Lord delighted in televising for the populace. Silvain will be the first, since you've relieved us of the possibility with the Lord."

"I'd toss Silvain right in there next to him, if I could." Then Inyx's voice quieted a little. "No, not that. Execute him, yes, I'd gladly do that. But punishment such as the Lord got should be reserved for the truly evil. Alberto Silvain is a pawn, a cunning one, in Claybore's game, and he poses only a minor threat."

"Is the subjugation of all the worlds along the Cenotaph Road a minor threat?" asked Lan. He felt little better for having been unconscious, but some measure of strength had trickled back. He survived on the edge, but that was better than being an inch beyond and cast into the dark abyss of unconsciousness.

"I'll not debate philosophy with you. The man's not to be found."

"He is still within the palace," said Lan. "Where, I can't say. But he's waiting for something."

"The cenotaph," spoke up Krek. "You remember the one we 'felt' yesterday?"

"Yesterday?" Lan sat upright, momentarily dizzy. "I've been asleep for an entire day?"

"A bit less. The cenotaph opened and closed. Perhaps he waits for it again."

"Where's the graveyard?" Lan demanded of Knoton. "I sense the openings and closings, but I'm too weak to pinpoint the exact cenotaph he'll use."

"I know where it is, friend Lan Martak. I have not been slumbering away my life while desperate characters like this Silvain rush about uncaptured."

"Take me there. Let's all get there. Don't waste time!" Lan cursed to himself all the way out of the palace and toward the back lawn. Inyx had to give him more support than he'd have liked. He vowed that the first thing he'd do when all this was behind them was rest for a week, then spend another week with Inyx in more enjoyable pursuits.

Afterward . . .

They made their way out into the neatly cropped lawn, down the path, and toward a small stand of trees. This close Lan "saw" the cenotaph—cenotaphs. No fewer than eight clustered in this minuscule graveyard.

"I've never seen so many in one place."

"Nor I," agreed the spider. "This is a world of strange contrasts. Obviously great courage is possible. Perhaps that goes with great evil, also."

"What are these cenotaphs?" asked Knoton. "You humans speak of them as if they were the most marvellous things in the world."

How could flesh and blood ever explain the concept of death to a mechanical? Or was it possible that mechs recognized disassembly in the same way? Lan didn't have the energy to explore the topic at the moment.

"They open gateways to other worlds. Claybore walks

the Cenotaph Road at will now, collecting hidden body artifacts. Silvain and others aid him; we oppose them.''

"Succinctly put," came Alberto Silvain's words. Lan spun, reaching for a death tube at his belt. His hand froze halfway there when he saw that Silvain aimed one of the weapons directly at Inyx's head. The commandant laughed, saying, ''So it's as I surmised. You'd face your own death willingly enough to stop me—and Claybore. But you won't risk hers. Claybore will find that interesting.''

"You know what he's trying to do," said Lan, trying to find the most convincing words. ''Join us, oppose him.''

"I side with the winners."

"Like the not very lamented Lord of the Twistings?" asked Krek.

"I had no choice in his case. Claybore ordered me to support him. Given the chance, I would have removed him permanently. I see that our lovely Inyx did that and more. She has a ruthlessness in her that I admire.''

"I'd rip out your liver and stuff it down your throat, if I could,'' the woman said, her tone low and menacing.

"See? Such an admirable display of courage. Too bad I must kill you all, before joining Claybore.''

"He's not doing too well regaining his tongue." Lan made it a statement, not a question.

"How'd you know—? Ah, a trick. There is no way you can know what happens on that world. You don't even know which world he's on. But as you have already learned from me, yes, progress is much too slow. I am now free to aid him. Then I shall return to this world and make it my own personal domain. He's promised me.''

"The cenotaph opens," said Krek.

Alberto Silvain jerked slightly in his eagerness to leave behind the world of his defeat. Inyx ducked, then rolled behind a gravestone. The death beam lashed out and blew the marker to tiny stone fragments. Silvain poised for a second shot when he saw Knoton, Krek, and Lan simultaneously starting for him. The odds were too great, the need to escape this world too binding.

He dived into the already opened crypt just inches under Lan's death beam.

Even as they approached, Lan Martak knew they were too late to stop the transition. Krek made a tiny choking noise, then sat down, legs akimbo around him.

"He is gone," lamented the spider. "He has walked the Cenotaph Road."

"It'll be a full day before we can follow, too, Curse the luck!"

"You would follow?" asked Knoton, in surprise. "But if the other side is like this one, why can't Silvain post a guard who will kill you as you emerge?"

"No reason in this world—or any world. We have to try to stop him, though. Claybore's evil makes the Lord of the Twistings look small in comparison."

The mechanical said nothing, studying the two humans and arachnid.

"Let's return to the palace," suggested Inyx. "We can prepare for the journey tomorrow."

As they walked back, illusions began popping up on the lawn. By the time they made their way into the audience chamber, Jonrod the Flash stood in the center of the stage, gesticulating wildly.

". . . and further, I promise you the most elaborate illusions known to magical conjuration. Your faith in me as your newly appointed Lord is not misplaced."

"What is this?" yelled Knoton. He glanced around. The other mechanicals stood silently along the walls. Humans crowded in close to the stage. "What right do you have to declare yourself Lord?"

Jonrod blinked, as if not believing his own eyes.

"You're a mechanical," he said. "I don't have to answer to you. But I will," he said hurriedly, when he saw the angry surge in the mechanical army. "I have spoken with the others who ran for the position. They agreed unanimously I am the best choice. Jonrod the Flash is new Lord of the Twistings!''

"There is no more Twistings," said Knoton.

"So? A Lord is still required to give the people what they need most." Illusions danced around the stage at Jonrod's feet.

"He's right, you know," said Lan. "There is a need for someone to fill the post."

"This man is irresponsible, a thief! He'd ruin not only Dicca but the entire planet during one single term of office." The mechanical was clearly outraged at the idea of Jonrod being elected to any position more responsible than grounds keeper.

"Oppose him. There ought to be an election. Let the people decide whether you or Jonrod is fit to rule. Remember, there are humans out there who bitterly opposed the former Lord and Silvain. I doubt they've been wiped out entirely. They'd support you."

The mech simply stared at Lan. Humans around the stage began to mutter, then one came over and slapped Knoton on the back.

"I'm getting pretty tired of the way things are done. Maybe you can change them. After all, Knokno's park is pretty damn good."

"I'd st—" Lan cut off the mechanical before he said anything that would ensure Jonrod's election.

"My friend was about to say he'd *start* opening the park to all the people. Can Jonrod match anything Knokno, a mechanical, creates?"

"Wait. I'm Lord. This is outrageous!" protested Jonrod.

"Elect Knoton!" came the cry from the perimeter of the room. The mechanicals who had followed Knoton in the Twistings, and the ones who had joined after his escape, all began cheering. Soon, many of the humans were, too.

"Very well," said Knoton with ill grace. "I'll run against him. But there will be changes if I'm elected Lord!"

Lan smiled as Knoton was swept up in the enthusiasm of the crowd. He turned to Inyx and Krek and said, "I'm sure there will be."

"It opens at any moment," said Krek, peering into the open crypt.

"How are we going to do this?" asked Inyx. "Claybore and Silvain are sure to have their soldiers waiting for us."

"Time flows differently between worlds. We might be able to arrive close enough on Silvain's heels that he hasn't had time to contact Claybore."

"A faint hope."

"Yes," Lan Martak admitted. "But still a hope." He and Inyx stood with arms around one another. The cenotaph began to glow, to open its gateway onto a new world. This time they'd walk the Cenotaph Road together.

Lan, Inyx, and Krek crowded forward to squeeze into the cenotaph on their way to adventure.

MORE SCIENCE FICTION!
ADVENTURE